Courtenay exhaled a shivering breath. 'I've read about men like you—ruthless men, who trample on anyone and anything in their way—but you're the first I've ever met.' She shook her head. 'I feel sorry for you.'

'Oh, please don't.' Graydon's tone was mild. 'I always get what I want, one way or another. Perhaps you haven't learned yet, as I did a long time ago, that money is what makes the world go round. Money, Ms West, is power.'

Another book you will enjoy
by GRACE GREEN

RISK OF THE HEART

This year Capri was determined to avoid her father's heavy-handed matchmaking attempts and have a proper holiday—one where for a short while she could experience a real change of lifestyle instead of constantly fighting off rich admirers. What she hadn't bargained on was Taggart Smith—a man who *was* to her liking. . .

WINTER DESTINY

BY

GRACE GREEN

DERBYSHIRE COUNTY COUNCIL

DERBYSHIRE
COUNTY LIBRARY
WITHDRAWN FROM STOCK
FOR SALE
-9 SEP 1991

6 50

F

Blagreaves

DATE ....

MILLS & BOON LIMITED
ETON HOUSE   18–24 PARADISE ROAD
RICHMOND   SURREY   TW9 1SR

All the characters in this book have no existence outside the imagination of the Author, and have no relation whatsoever to anyone bearing the same name or names. They are not even distantly inspired by any individual known or unknown to the Author, and all the incidents are pure invention.

All Rights Reserved. The text of this publication or any part thereof may not be reproduced or transmitted in any form or by any means, electronic or mechanical, including photocopying, recording, storage in an information retrieval system, or otherwise, without the written permission of the publisher.

MILLS & BOON and Rose Device is registered in U.S. Patent and Trademark Office.

*First published in Great Britain 1991
by Mills & Boon Limited*

© Grace Green 1991

Australian copyright 1991

ISBN 0 263 12909 8

*Set in 10 on 11 pt Linotron Baskerville
07-9109-57659
Typeset in Great Britain by Centracet, Cambridge
Made and printed in Great Britain*

TO MY DAUGHTER MARGARET

CHAPTER ONE

His search was over.

She was so close that he could almost smell the sultry perfume her kind of woman would wear.

He eased the Mercedes along Lakeshore Boulevard, slowing as he came to the four-thousand block. Winding down his window so that he could see more clearly in the near-pitch-black night, he felt his cheeks stung by the wind whistling inland from across the frozen lake, its keening sound almost blotting out the squeak of his tyres on the packed snow.

God, but he was tired! With the back of one hand he rubbed the grittiness from his eyes as he drove along, searching the shadows for street numbers.

Forty-two thirty-four, forty-two thirty-six, forty-two thirty-eight. . .

His heart thudded heavily beneath his charcoal-grey sweater as he found the number he was looking for.

Forty-two forty.

A lone street-light adjacent to the house revealed a two-storey wooden building, snow piled high on the roof, icicles daggering from the eaves.

For a moment, he wondered if he should park further along, but then, with an abrupt shrug, he pulled in at the kerb. The place was in darkness—and, even if she saw the car, she would have no way of knowing whose it was.

He switched off the headlights, and, reaching into the pocket of his leather jacket, took out his wallet and opened it. The photo behind the plastic window was only a two-by-three-inch snap, but it was clearly focused.

He slid it out and held it above the steering-wheel. The rays slanting through the windscreen from the street lamp were yellow, and they made her flowing hair appear even more blonde, gave her chiselled features a sallow tinge, made her slender figure look as if it was carved from butter.

'To Patrick, forever, Courtenay.'

A contemptuous smile twisted his mouth as he traced a fingertip over the full swell of her breasts.

Courtenay.

The other woman.

The term was clichéd, but so was her image: a beautiful, selfish blonde. Normally the type he avoided like the plague.

But this one had something he wanted. And when he wanted something, he didn't rest till he got it.

It was the beginning of December now. If everything went as smoothly as he expected, before the New Year he and Alanna would be hearing childish laughter ringing through the lonely rooms at Seacliffe House.

As he turned the key in the ignition and pulled away from the kerb, the tiredness cleared from his eyes and they became steel-hard.

Tomorrow he would set his plan in motion.

'The first Noel the angels did say. . .'

Courtenay West sang the words of her favourite Christmas carol under her breath as she folded a pile of red and green paper napkins for tomorrow afternoon's office party. Outside her window, she could hear gales of laughter as a group of workers passed on their way from the Mom's Own Bakery warehouse to the company cafeteria. Though Christmas was still a couple of days away, the holiday spirit was in the air, and had been for several weeks.

She had caught it herself—and not only here at Mom's Own, but at home, with Vicky. She found herself chuckling as she thought of all the plans the two of them had made for the festive season, and of the fun they'd had making them. Who would have guessed more than nine years ago that her pregnancy, which had caused her so much anguish then, would have ended up bringing her so much happiness? To think that in the very darkest moments of her despair, when she had discovered how Patrick had betrayed her, she had actually considered giving up her baby for adoption. . . She shuddered. She could not even *imagine* life now without Vicky——

'Courtenay!'

She glanced up with a start as she heard her name shrieked from the corridor, and was in time to see Krystle, one of the junior typists, barrelling through the open doorway of the small office, her cheeks flushed to the colour of holly berries.

Whirling to a halt in front of Courtenay's desk, the chubby brunette announced in a breathless rush, 'You'll never guess!'

'I'll never guess what?' Courtenay pushed aside her thoughts of her daughter and arched a questioning brow at her co-worker.

Krystle's brown eyes glittered with excitement. 'The new man has arrived!'

'He has?' Folding the last napkin, Courtenay asked in a teasing tone, 'And which new man would we be talking about?'

'The new owner of Mom's Own, of course!'

'Krystle!' Courtenay frowned warningly as her gaze flickered to the open doorway, and she lowered her voice as she added, 'Mr Ketterton has never so much as *hinted* that he's sold the company—it's nothing but a wild rumour!'

Krystle hitched up her purple suede skirt and parked her plump bottom stubbornly on Courtenay's desk. 'If it's just a wild rumour, then where did Mr K. get the cash to modernise the plant? Everybody knows that at the beginning of December he was teetering on the edge of bankruptcy, and now—just three weeks later—the old ovens have been ripped out and replaced with state-of-the-art computerised equipment and——'

'This "new man". . .' Courtenay ruthlessly stemmed Krystle's speculative flow. 'Did you see him yourself, or did your information come via the office grapevine?'

'Oh, I saw him!' Krystle uttered an ecstatic moan. 'He was striding along the corridor towards Mr K.'s office, in a magnificent black leather jacket. Tall, dark, and absolutely devastating. He has the sexiest scowl, and——' she began ticking off the stranger's other attributes with a nail-bitten finger '—jet black hair, a Palm Springs tan, eyes the colour of peacock feathers——'

'*Peacock feathers*?' Courtenay didn't try to hide her scepticism.

'Yes,' responded Krystle firmly. 'Peacock feathers. And I,' she announced, sliding off her perch, 'am going to prepare a tray of coffee, because I know Mr K. is going to offer him refreshments. This man is *somebody*!'

Courtenay shook her head reprovingly as she arranged the folded napkins in a neat pile. 'You're jumping to conclusions, Krystle. Just because you see a good-looking man in the building, it doesn't follow that he's bought the company.'

'It's not just his looks. . .' The clink of china and silverware accompanied Krystle's response as she rummaged in the cupboard of the office's small kitchen area.

'It's—oh, it's just something *about* him. Wait till you see him—he positively oozes money, and power, and——'

The shrill ring of the phone interrupted the enthusiastic outpouring, and Courtenay sent up a silent prayer of thanks. With a murmured 'Excuse me', she lifted the receiver.

'Courtenay?' Her employer's voice boomed in her ear.

'Yes, Mr Ketterton?'

'Coffee for two in my office, please.'

So the man *was* somebody! 'Krystle's preparing a tray.' Courtenay met the typist's questioning look with a nod and a wry smile. 'She'll be right there.'

'No, Courtenay, I want *you* to bring it in.'

Courtenay blinked in surprise, and slowly replaced the receiver. How very odd! Since Alf had elevated her six months ago from her previous secretarial position to her present post as his administrative assistant, he'd never once asked her to make coffee for him.

'I was right?' Krystle licked her lips with the tip of her tongue as if she were a kitten anticipating a bowl of cream.

Courtenay rolled back her computer chair and stood up. 'Only half right, I'm afraid. His lordship does want coffee, but I'm to do the honours.'

'Oh, drat! Once Mr Tall, Dark and Devastating sets eyes on you, he'll look no further.'

Courtenay laughed as she lifted the steaming coffee carafe on to the tray. 'Perhaps he doesn't like blondes!'

'And perhaps he doesn't like huge sea-green eyes and legs that start under the armpits either!'

'You know I'm not interested in men.' Despite the warmth in the centrally heated office, Courtenay suddenly felt chilled as memories of Patrick slid into her mind. With an effort, she blocked out the images, and even managed a dismissive smile.

'You may not be interested in men, but that doesn't

stop them being interested in you.' Pouting, Krystle threw herself down on to Courtenay's chair. 'Why is it that people always want what they can't have? You'd think your having a nine-year-old kid would be enough to scare men off, but it doesn't. The only guy around here who isn't panting for you is old Alf—and that's because to him and Flo you're like the daughter they never had!'

As Courtenay walked along the corridor to Alf's office a couple of minutes later, she sighed wearily. Krystle was right. Men did find her attractive—they seemed to be fascinated by her ash-blonde hair and her full, high breasts—but there was nothing she could do about it. Or rather, she amended, she had done all she could, but it hadn't made any difference! At work she always wore her hair swept up in a topknot, and played down her curves by dressing in crisp shirts and tailored skirts. But it seemed that the more businesslike and unapproachable the image she tried to project, the more of a challenge men seemed to find her. . .

As she reached her employer's door, she resolutely switched her thoughts to the moments that lay ahead. Giving the coffee tray a quick glance to make sure nothing had been forgotten, she inhaled a deep steadying breath. If Krystle happened to be right, and this man, this dark stranger, was the new owner of Mom's Own, she wanted to make a good impression. Her job was all-important to her. A single mother in her position couldn't afford to be out of work.

After a brisk knock, she opened the door.

'Ah, come in, Courtenay.' Alf Ketterton was sitting behind his desk, his pale face flushed, his normally jovial expression serious. 'Put it right here.' He brushed aside a heap of files.

Out of the corner of her eye, Courtenay could see Krystle's 'new man'. He was leaning indolently against the wall by the window, hands in trouser pockets, legs crossed at the ankles, in a typically male, typically arrogant pose.

An uneasy shiver skimmed the surface of her skin as she laid down the tray. The atmosphere in Alf's office was usually relaxed and low-key. This morning she could feel all sorts of unfamiliar vibes in the air. If it weren't crazy, she could have sworn those vibes were crackling with hostility.

'Shall I pour, Mr Ketterton?' Her voice was low-pitched and professional.

'Thank you, Courtenay.'

As she set out the mugs, she could sense the stranger's penetrating gaze on her back. She could almost feel it, as if there were fingers running over her upswept blonde hair, her slender waist, the curve of her hip. Well, he wouldn't find anything amiss, she told herself with a defiant tightening of her lips. . .and felt inexplicably pleased that she was wearing her best grey skirt with the discreet kick-pleat, and that she'd ironed her white cotton shirt so fastidiously the night before.

She turned to ask him how he liked his coffee, and as their gazes met she felt her stomach muscles clench.

Peacock feathers. Krystle was right about the colour of his eyes! They were an incredible blue-green, fringed with outrageously long, thick lashes. . .

And they were fixed on her coldly, as if he were examining a particularly nasty insect under a microscope!

She almost staggered back a step. This man didn't like her! They'd never met before—she'd have remembered those eyes!—yet there was no mistaking the contempt in his gaze. What on earth had she done to warrant such animosity?

Despite her bewilderment and dismay, she managed

to keep her voice steady as she asked, 'How do you like your coffee, sir?'

His response was curt. 'Black, please.'

She had a fleeting, blurred image of a dark business suit, an icy white shirt, and a perfectly knotted red tie, before she turned away again, her heart thumping like a hammer against her ribcage. No wonder Krystle had been so impressed! This man had a raw, powerful sexuality that pulled at her with invisible hands. Even at six paces, she could feel the impact of his magnetism.

Somehow she managed to walk across the room without tripping, though her legs had become strangely weak. And though she tried to avoid touching him as she gave him his coffee, somehow their fingers brushed together, and, though it was a mere brushing of skin against skin, it sent a jolting electric sensation shooting right through her.

Feeling as shocked as if she'd touched a live cable, Courtenay backed away. Nothing like that had ever happened to her before. . . Vaguely she was aware of the stranger's 'Thank you, Ms West,' and even more vaguely she was aware that his voice was exactly as she would have expected it to be—deep, educated, and slightly rasping.

Not until she was handing her employer his mug did she notice the man had called her Ms West, and as she did, she felt herself freeze. Alf always called her Courtenay—why would he have told his visitor her surname? Why would the man have wanted to know? *Was* he the new owner of Mom's Own?

She swivelled her head round involuntarily.

The stranger had straightened, and his mug was at his lips. His eyes were still on her—all at once more blue than green, a glacial blue that sent a message of arrogant, mocking challenge. She could tell, from his expression, that he knew exactly what she was thinking;

she could feel goose-bumps rising on her arms as she tore her gaze away.

'Will that be all, Mr Ketterton?'

'Fine, thanks, Courtenay.'

Courtenay excused herself and hurried from the room, her legs now like rubber, her pulses galloping out of control. Closing the door behind her, she leaned her head back against it, feeling the harsh throb of her skull against the polished wood.

She had no idea how long she stood there, barely aware of the hum of the men's voices beyond the door, before eventually pushing herself away. Like an automaton, she began walking along the corridor. But instead of heading straight back to the office, she detoured to the ladies' room; she couldn't face Krystle's inevitable, inquisitive questions. Not yet. . .

Relieved to see there was no one around, she slumped down into one of the two vinyl armchairs under the long mirror and tried to figure out just what was going on.

The only reason she could come up with for Alf having called her to bring in the coffee was to give the stranger an opportunity to inspect her. And he *had* inspected her. . .very thoroughly. . .

She flung herself to her feet and began pacing restlessly back and forth in the bare, white-tiled room, her thoughts whirling around chaotically.

She had worked for seven years at Mom's Own. Seven pleasant, uneventful years. Apart from the recent worry that the plant might close because the equipment kept breaking down and Alf apparently had no money to replace it, things had gone on month after month in the same old way.

But that was going to change. She knew it.

Something was going to happen; the feeling was in the air. She'd felt it the moment she'd gone into Alf's office. And it was going to happen soon. At this time of year, Millar's Lake was a sleepy little town. In the summer it was busy, bustling with tourists, but right now, just before Christmas, it was dead as the proverbial dodo.

When a man like the stranger in Alf's office came to a place like Millar's Lake, at this time of the year, it could only spell trouble for someone. And Courtenay had a horrible suspicion, from the way this particular stranger had challenged her with his mocking blue-green eyes, who that someone was going to be.

She was tidying up her desk before leaving for home when Alf came into the office with her pay envelope. When she glanced at her cheque she saw, to her bewilderment, that it was for more than twice the usual amount. An unfamiliar pink and white form was also enclosed; unfolding it, she saw that it was her Record of Employment. She scanned it with disbelieving eyes.

'I'm *fired*?' She couldn't have felt more winded if a horse had just kicked her in the chest.

'Not fired, Courtenay. . . Laid off. I'm trimming the staff—down-sizing, I believe, is the current buzz-word. As you can see, I've given you two weeks' pay in lieu of notice.' Shamefacedly, he slid his gaze from Courtenay's. 'January's only just around the corner, and you know how slow things are then. If business picks up later on, perhaps. . .' His words trailed away, and they hung falsely in the air between them. Guilty colour stained his cheeks as, finally, he met Courtenay's eyes again.

Numb with shock, she could only stare at him. Laid off. . .fired. . .what was the difference? Either way, it meant no pay-cheque coming in. . . 'I don't understand,' she whispered at last. 'Why me? Or are you laying off some others?'

'No, just you. Courtenay, I'm sorry. I didn't want to

do this, but I had no choice. It was either that or. . .' Alf broke off, biting his lip as if he'd started to say something, then decided he couldn't finish.

Courtenay swallowed back words of protest as she realised that, whatever the reason behind Alf's move, he was finding this just as difficult as she was. 'Don't worry, Alf,' she said wearily. 'I know you wouldn't be firing me unless you had to. These things happen. It's just that. . .well, I know you were having financial problems, but I thought—I thought the situation must have turned around somehow, with the new equipment. . .'

Alf walked heavily across to her and put his arms round her. 'I'm so sorry, Courtenay, dear. If there'd been any other way. . . I wish you all the best, and I hope you'll keep in touch with Flo and me. We've come to love you very much. . .'

Courtenay put her arms round his bulky waist. 'Oh, Alf, of course I'll keep in touch.' Impulsively, she stood on her tiptoe and brushed his jaw with a fleeting kiss. 'I love you too. . .'

Alf had his back to the door, and a small sound behind him startled Courtenay. Frowning, she tilted her chin and looked over his broad shoulder, and when she saw the tall figure outside in the corridor she felt her heartbeats stagger; it was the visitor who had been in Alf's office that morning. She hadn't heard his footsteps, so absorbed had she been in what she'd been saying.

But now, as she stood there in her employer's embrace, and saw the sneer curling the stranger's upper lip, she realised with a jolt how the scene must look. But as she drew back, the dark figure moved away again, and a moment later she heard his footsteps fading along the corridor.

Alf obviously hadn't noticed anything. He patted her shoulder gently, then, with a murmured, ''Bye,

Courtenay. Perhaps we'll see you over the holidays. . .' he left.

Hardly knowing what she was doing, Courtenay opened the bottom drawer of her desk and pulled out a large plastic bag. How could a day that had started out so well have ended so disastrously? Only hours ago she'd been looking forward to the Christmas break. Now she would have to spend the time looking for a job. And where was she going to find another job at this time of year? No one hired over the holidays——

She paused, staring into space. Alf had looked so guilty. Was it possible that he had been lying, that he wasn't really down-sizing? That he'd used that as an excuse to get rid of her? But *why*? She had never known him to lie before; and until today she would have staked her life on it that he would never lie to *her*.

Her head began to spin as she tried to sort out the events of the day. Everything had been fine till. . .till the moment she'd set eyes on the dark stranger.

Was it possible that her dismissal was connected in some way with his visit? Had he somehow influenced Alf? He'd made no secret of his hostility towards her.

Tightening her lips, she stuffed all her personal possessions into the plastic bag. It didn't really make any difference, did it? Whatever the reason, she had lost her job. And if word got around that Alf had fired her— as it surely would in this small town—she would have no hope of getting another one. Not only was Alf owner of Mom's Own, he was also town mayor—and a very influential town mayor at that.

Distractedly Courtenay unhooked her shoulder-bag from the back of her chair. She didn't have time to stand there, trying to come up with answers to all the questions buzzing around in her head. She had to get home—she'd promised Vicky they'd do some last-minute Christmas shopping together. She put on her coat and looked around one last time. Then, shaking her head dazedly, she crossed the office and went out into the foyer.

Marge, the receptionist, was putting on her coat, and they left the sprawling brick building together. As they walked down the steps, holding on to the rail so that their feet wouldn't slip on the snow-covered ice, a black Mercedes pulled out from a parking spot on the other side of the street. It glided away into the dark, its tyres making a squeaking sound on the snow.

'Now, that's my kind of car,' the receptionist said with a yearning sigh. 'Not often we see one of those in Millar's Lake. At least, not in the off-season—but funnily enough that's the second one I've seen today. Alf had a visitor this morning who drove a gorgeous black Merc. Probably you didn't notice it—it was parked at my side of the building.'

The wind was icy, and Courtenay pulled up the fake fur collar of her jacket to protect her warm cheeks. She had felt a *frisson* of apprehension run down her spine when she saw the car—for just a second she'd had a glimpse of the driver, and she had recognised the dark stranger. Why had he been hanging around the plant?

'Who was he, Marge?' she asked, in a deliberately casual tone. 'Or is it a big secret?'

Marge laughed. 'No secret. He told me his name when he asked me to call Alf and tell him he was on his way in.' The receptionist paused as she waved to her boyfriend, who had just drawn up alongside the kerb in a green truck. 'There's Rob—sorry, I've gotta go. See you tomorrow.'

'Marge!' Courtenay caught her arm as she moved away. 'Just a sec. I won't see you tomorrow. Alf has. . .let me go.'

'What?' Marge gaped at her. 'Why on earth———?'

'I think it might have something to do with that man who came to see Alf this morning. Who is he, Marge?'

'Why, his name's Winter—Graydon Winter. Did you happen to see the article about him in last week's *Vancouver Standard*? "Rich, Reclusive, Ruthless". No photo—that's because he's reclusive, I guess! He's the founder and president of Ocean-West, Vancouver's biggest shipping company——' A raucous toot from the green truck had the receptionist grimacing, and then, with a sincere, 'I'm real sorry you've been let go, Courtenay. Call me—we'll have lunch some time,' Marge was off at a run, her boots thudding on the snow.

Courtenay stumbled to the bus shelter a few yards away, and as she sank down on the bench she felt as if every drop of blood was draining from her veins. Graydon Winter. Oh, dear God. . .

What was Patrick's brother doing in Millar's Lake?

Did he know who she was? Had he learned of her affair with Patrick? Was he aware that she had given birth to Patrick's child?

Courtenay felt a dreadful clawing fear constricting her heart, and she dared not face the most terrifying question of all.

Had he come to Millar's Lake to try to take Vicky from her?

CHAPTER TWO

COURTENAY'S rented basement flat was in darkness when she hurried round the corner from the bus-stop twenty minutes later. She uttered an impatient exclamation. She had left the outside light on as usual when she left for work in the morning; it must have burned out during the day.

Once inside, she made straight for the living-room. Throwing down her jacket, she crossed to the old-fashioned brick fireplace, which was decorated with pine cones and Christmas cards, and under the vase of paper holly Vicky had made in school she found what she was looking for.

She sank down on the sofa and spread the dog-eared cutting on her lap. She didn't really have to read the obituary—she knew it off by heart. But now that Graydon Winter was in town she felt compelled to look at it again.

Patrick Winter, vice-president of Ocean-West Shipping, Vancouver, and his wife Elizabeth, died July 3rd, in a yachting accident in the Caribbean. The couple, who had no children, had been married 17 years. Patrick is survived by his mother, Alanna, and his elder brother Graydon. Funeral July 8th, at Cedars Cemetery, West Vancouver.

Courtenay could still recall the shock she'd felt when she had happened on the obituary in the newspaper six months ago and had found out that Patrick was dead. . .but she'd felt no grief, even though he had been the father of her child. And she felt no grief now.

21

Bitterness was all she felt, a corroding bitterness that had begun nine and a half years ago when she'd found out the truth about Patrick, a bitterness that since then had eaten deeply into her heart. She had sworn that no man would ever use her again. . .

How could she have let him dupe her the way he had? How could she have been so blind, so foolish?

But even as she asked herself the questions—questions she had asked herself a thousand times before—she knew the answer. She'd succumbed to Patrick's charm because she had been starved for love.

She had only been a toddler when her mother had died, and she'd been brought up by a father who had had no time for her. After all these years, she still felt an ache in her heart as she recalled the desperate way she had tried to win his affection—recalled the despair when she suffered the inevitable harsh rejection.

Her last years in high school had been utterly miserable. Her father had remarried when she was fourteen, and he and Courtenay's stepmother had warned her that as soon as she graduated she would have to move out and support herself. They made no secret of the fact that as far as they were concerned that day couldn't come soon enough.

So after graduation she moved from her home town of Kelowna to Whistler, where she found a job as a clerk in one of the popular ski resort's exclusive hotels. And about six months later, Patrick Winter—blue-eyed, auburn-haired, charming—had swept into her life. He had come to Whistler from Vancouver for a skiing weekend with a group of friends, and when he told her he was a commercial traveller, she had no reason to disbelieve him. Within days, he convinced her he had fallen in love with her, and Courtenay's heart had opened to him like a bud flowering in the sun.

That he wouldn't speak about his family hadn't

bothered her; she'd had no inclination to talk about hers either.

He had wanted her desperately, had groaned that he was obsessed by her slender, curvy body, her long blonde hair. . .

Though it had all happened a long time ago, she could still recall her embarrassment when she had told him she loved him too, but that she didn't believe in pre-marital sex.

Over several weeks, on his frequent visits to Whistler, he had alternately argued, coaxed, and pleaded, telling her over and over that she could depend on him, promising her she could trust him. But she hadn't given in.

He had married her then. . .

Or so she had thought——

The sound of a door slamming jarred Courtenay back to the present. 'Vicky?' she called breathlessly.

'Where are you, Mom?'

'In here.'

'Hi!' Her daughter's cheerily shouted response preceded her into the living-room. 'I've been walking Snoopy for Mrs Albert. Look what she gave me!' The slight figure, clad in jeans and an emerald-green snow-jacket that set off her short russet curls, kicked off her boots and padded across the thin carpet to her mother.

As Courtenay put the newspaper cutting on the arm of the chesterfield, she saw Vicky glance at it. The child made no comment, but opened her small hand to reveal a jingle of coins. Swallowing in an effort to relieve the tightness in her throat caused by her journey into the past, Courtenay looked at her daughter's wind-flushed face—at the turned-up nose, the wide smile with its slight overbite, the sparkling blue eyes—and felt her heart melt with love. What a very sweet and dear child she was; not the prettiest in the world, she admitted honestly, probably not even the brightest. But without a doubt she was the most lovable. . .

And she was the spitting image of her father.

What would Graydon Winter say if he could see her? Again Courtenay felt the dreadful clawing fear that had constricted her heart earlier. He was so wealthy, so powerful—the kind of man who would stop at nothing to achieve his goals. . .

'Are you going to put it in your bank?' she asked, her voice husky as she fought to control her feelings of panic.

'Some of it.' Vicky slid the money into her pocket. 'I'm going to spend the rest when we go shopping tonight.'

'Vicky. . .' Courtenay hesitated. She didn't want to spoil her daughter's mood by telling her of the day's events, but it would be better to get it over with.

'What is it, Mom?'

'A couple of things have happened that you should know about,' she said steadily. 'First of all. . .' she brushed the back of one hand gently over Vicky's freckled cheek '. . . I've lost my job.'

'Oh, Mom!' Vicky sat down on the couch and Courtenay felt a pair of cold hands slide round her neck—hands that had a definite doggy smell. 'Don't worry. You'll find something else—we'll manage till then. And we can use the special money put by for when I start going to the orthodontist if things get really rough! But they won't.'

Courtenay wished she could share her daughter's optimism. 'There's something else. A man came to the office today, to talk with Mr Ketterton. I found out later—he's your uncle, Graydon Winter.'

'My *uncle*?' Vicky's blue gaze slid to the cutting. 'Is that why you were looking at the obituary?'

When Patrick had died, Courtenay had sat down with Vicky and told her of his death. Courtenay could still recall how the colour had drained from the little face, could still hear her daughter's pleading words, 'I've *got* to go to the funeral! I never met him, so he's never seemed real to me—he's been like someone in a story-book. Just make-believe. If I see him being buried, then he'd be real to me. I'd know I did have a real father.'

Courtenay's heart had twisted with pain. Vicky had grown up fatherless, but she'd always acted as if she didn't care. Courtenay had never suspected the depth of the deprivation in the young heart. She had pulled her daughter's tense little body into her arms and held her tightly.

'I'm sorry,' she'd whispered, stroking the russet curls. 'We can't go. His mother is sure to be at the funeral, and his brother. You're so like your father; they might guess who you were—it would upset them dreadfully.'

Finally Vicky had said in a choking voice, 'All right, Mom, I understand.'

And she had never mentioned it again, though several times Courtenay had found her reading the obituary.

Now Courtenay said quietly, 'Yes, that's why I'm looking at it. Seeing him made me think about your father.'

'Now. . .' she got up and walked with brisk steps across the room '. . .let's have dinner. And before we go out I'm going to prepare a Thermos of hot chocolate. We'll put on a log when we come home, and sit by the fire while we wrap the presents. How does that sound?'

'Fine.' Vicky's voice was muffled. 'Mom. . .'

'Yes?' Courtenay paused, her fingers gripping the edge of the door as she looked round. 'What is it?'

'Why is Uncle Graydon here? In Millar's Lake? Do you think he's going to pay us a visit?'

Courtenay felt her pulse begin to hammer just as it had that afternoon when she'd fled from Alf's office and the dark stranger's disturbing presence. She turned away so that Vicky wouldn't be able to see the dread in her eyes, and called over her shoulder, 'I don't know, honey. We shall just have to wait and see.'

A black Mercedes was parked outside the house when they returned from their shopping trip.

They were almost at the gate before Courtenay noticed it, but, even as she felt the blood chill in her veins, she realised the sleekly luxurious vehicle was empty.

And almost immediately after she noticed that it wasn't the only car in the street that didn't belong. There were other unfamiliar vehicles parked nearby, and the long driveway of the house next door looked like a used car lot.

She expelled a shaky breath. Of course—the Alberts had relatives coming from out of town for a Christmas family reunion. The driver of the Mercedes must be one of them.

'Hurry up, Mom. What are you staring at?' Vicky's voice was impatient. 'My feet are freezing!'

With a last look at the empty car, Courtenay said, 'Coming,' and walked slowly to join the bouncing figure at the end of the path, ordering her heartbeats to stop racing.

'Are we going to light the log, Mom, and have our hot chocolate by the fire?'

Courtenay clicked the garden gate shut behind them. 'We are. And then we'll wrap our presents——'

'You'll never guess what I've bought you. Can I show you tonight? You know how I hate waiting——'

'*May* I show you. And yes, I know how you hate waiting, but no, you *may* not show me tonight! You don't hate waiting as much as I love——'

'*May* I open the door, Mom?' Vicky interrupted with a giggle. '*Please* give me your key.'

'Watch you don't trip. I should have taken the time to replace that burned-out bulb before we went shopping.' Courtenay rummaged in her bag as they turned the corner, her eyes straining in the dark. 'Ah, here they are.'

She rattled her keys and fumbled to find Vicky's hand. 'As I was saying, Miss Impatience, if there's one thing I like better than anything in the world it's a surprise.'

A split second after she spoke, she felt the hair rise at her nape. There was someone standing right beside her in the shadows. A man. She could see his tall shape, smell his male scent, hear his deep steady breathing. She turned to reach for Vicky, a scream gathering in her throat, but before she could make a sound a strong hand gripped her arm, and a familiar, mocking voice grated in her ear.

'So you like surprises. Now isn't that lucky, Ms West, because I have one helluva surprise for you.'

For a brief moment Courtenay thought she was going to pass out; her body felt as bloodless as that of Vicky's snowman standing rigidly in the centre of the front lawn. So Graydon Winter *had* come to Millar's Lake to look for her. She had prayed she was mistaken; now she knew her fears had been justified. Gathering herself together with a sudden surge of inner strength, she wrenched her arm free.

'Don't touch me!' She put out a hand blindly, searching for Vicky. 'Honey, give me the key.'

'It's all right, Mom.' Vicky's voice was high with excitement. 'I've got it!'

The door creaked open, and, switching on the passage light, Vicky led the way through to the kitchen. Courtenay compressed her lips into a thin line as the outside door clicked shut behind her. Obviously Graydon Winter wasn't about to wait for an invitation to enter.

Flinging her packages on the kitchen table, she turned angrily to confront him, and, as she did, she almost reeled back from the impact of his presence.

He was wearing the black leather jacket Krystle had raved about, but he had discarded the business suit in favour of a black crewneck sweater and black cords which accentuated the lean, muscled length of his frame. The wind had swept his hair back from his face, revealing hard, grim features, and in the kitchen's unforgiving fluorescent lighting his unshaven jaw looked as if someone had scraped charcoal over its strong planes. His image was stunningly harsh, like that of a dark, ruthless executioner.

'What do you want?' Courtenay looked at him challengingly, but as her gaze locked with his she felt a jolt of shock. If a person's eyes were the windows of his soul, then Graydon Winter's soul was indeed in a state of profound turmoil. She could see anger in the blue-green depths, she could see hostility, and she could see a bleak contempt—but she could also see another emotion, one which caused her heartbeats to pound in dismay. It wasn't the first time she had seen desire in a man's eyes, but what she detected in Graydon Winter's eyes was more than desire. It was a deep, savage hunger. . .

But even as she stared, stunned, the look vanished. And it disappeared with such speed that she wondered if it had been there at all. She closed her eyes briefly. Perhaps she'd imagined it. . .but surely not, for the involuntary response it had stimulated in every erotic pulse in her body was so real, so intense, that she felt as if she was on fire.

When she looked at him again, she found to her relief that he was no longer staring at her. He was openly inspecting the shabby kitchen, and his gaze—utterly devoid of the disturbing emotions she had seen there moments before—was now hard and critical. She

struggled to control a sudden surge of resentment, but
when he rubbed the toe of one shoe over a hole in the
worn lino and she saw the scornful curl of his upper lip
she lost the battle.

'Have you something to say,' she snapped, 'or have
you come to examine the place for cockroaches?'

Vicky looked uncertainly from her mother to their
visitor and back to Courtenay again. 'Shall I pour the
hot chocolate, Mom?' she asked in a placating tone. 'I
think there's enough for the three of us.'

'Your daughter seems to have more manners than her
mother.' Graydon flung her a taunting look. 'Isn't it
customary to offer refreshments on such a cold night?'

Encouraged, Vicky extended her invitation further.
'Mom's going to light a log—we can all sit by the fire.
Should I light it now, Mom?'

'Our guest won't be staying, Vicky. After he's gone
we'll——'

'You refer to me as your guest.' Graydon slid his
hands into the pockets of his black cords and Courtenay
heard the clink of keys. 'Why don't you tell your
daughter who I am, or don't you know? Am I over-
estimating the efficiency of the office grapevine at
Mom's Own?'

'Oh, the office grapevine is working like clockwork.'
Courtenay's tone was derisive as she went on, 'You're
the rich, reclusive, ruthless Graydon Winter, president
of Ocean-West, Vancouver's largest shipping company!'

Before he could respond, Vicky piped up delightedly,
'I was right! You are my uncle, aren't you? My dad's
brother?'

'Vicky——' Courtenay felt her arm tremble as she
hurriedly sloshed hot chocolate into a mug and replaced
the lid on the Thermos '—I want you to go to your
room while I talk to Mr Winter——'

'But, Mom——'

'No buts!' Courtenay put on her no-nonsense voice, and saw Vicky's little chest heave frustratedly under her green sweater. 'Excuse me for a moment.' She didn't look directly at the man she was addressing, but from the corner of her eye she could see him take the lid from the Thermos. 'Make yourself at home!' she added in a sarcastic tone.

Vicky's bedroom was at the other end of the flat from the kitchen, and the child didn't speak as they walked along the narrow hallway together, but as soon as they were in her room, she slammed the door with such force that the draught dislodged several of the doggy posters pinned to the walls.

'Why can't I stay?' she demanded. 'He's my uncle.'

'I'm sorry, Vicky.' Courtenay laid the mug of hot chocolate on the nightstand. 'I want you to remain in your room. I promise that when our visitor leaves I'll tell you everything.' Slipping off her coat, she laid it across the foot of the bed before tossing her hat beside it.

'Why is he so mad at you?' Vicky's blue gaze moved dully towards the closed door. 'What did *you* do?'

Courtenay caught sight of herself in the dresser mirror, and with a distracted sigh, dragged her fingers through her dishevelled hair in a vain attempt to tidy it. Her cheeks were flushed, her eyes too bright, her lips trembling. She made a soft sound of distress, and, turning back to Vicky, murmured, 'Honey, I have to go.' She waited for a moment to see if Vicky had anything more to say, but her daughter just threw herself sulkily on to the bed and twisted her face away.

Stepping out into the hallway, Courtenay closed the door and leaned against it for a moment, her body feeling rubbery as waves of faintness rolled over her. She drew the back of one hand over her brow and found her skin moist with perspiration. What did Graydon Winter want?

Well, she wasn't going to find out if she stayed here in the corridor! Taking a deep breath, she walked back to the kitchen, to find that he had draped his jacket over one of the bentwood chairs and was standing at the other side of the table, his hands wrapped around a steaming mug.

She felt her throat tighten. It was a small kitchen, but she had never before noticed just how small it was. He seemed to fill it with his presence; the very air was alive with the dynamic raw power vibrating from him. She'd heard the expression 'larger than life', but she'd never been sure what it meant. She knew now. . .and the knowledge only added to the fear building up inside her.

She clenched her hands into fists at her side. 'How dare you come barging into our lives? And to do it in such an underhand way. You could give someone a heart attack, hiding in the dark like that!' She saw his gaze move over her, and desperately wished she was still wearing her businesslike office outfit, not this knit dress that clung to her curves and was the same sea-green as her eyes——

There was no mistaking the sexual awareness in his expression as his gaze lingered on her silky blonde hair and the rich swell of her breasts. Courtenay felt an unfamiliar heat coiling round inside her as if he had actually woven his long fingers through the shining strands, actually caressed her flesh with his——

'I didn't intend to startle you.' His gaze was, incredibly, once again cold and shuttered as it moved back to trap her own. 'I'd only just arrived, had just rung your bell, as a matter of fact, when you came around the corner. I don't get my kicks out of terrifying unprotected females. I could have approached you when you left work this afternoon—would you have preferred to have our meeting in the street, with your co-worker looking on?'

'I really have nothing to say to you.' Courtenay felt a vague throbbing begin around her temples. 'Please tell me what you want and leave.'

He raised his mug to his lips and swallowed a mouthful of his chocolate drink. When he looked at her again, the steely glint in his eyes cut into her like the blade of a newly sharpened knife. 'I want Victoria.'

Courtenay felt her knees begin to buckle under her, and she placed an unsteady hand on the chairback in front of her for support. 'You must be out of your mind!' She couldn't keep a tremor from her voice. 'Vicky is *my daughter*. Why on earth would you think I'd be willing to give her up?'

'The answer to that is simple. I can offer her a better life.'

'Vicky and I have a perfectly good life here.' Courtenay drew on all her self-control and noticed thankfully that her voice no longer trembled. 'Not as fancy as your own life in Vancouver, of course, but Millar's Lake is a nice town, and this flat is quite adequate for——'

'This place may be quite adequate for *you*, but it's certainly not adequate for any niece of mine. Oh, I realise rented places are almost impossible to come by in this part of the world, and you were glad to get it when you moved here seven years ago, but even this one will be out of your league now. . .'

Courtenay stared, speechless, as she listened to him. How much did he know about her? Too much, she guessed.

'You have a loan at the bank that you incurred two years ago when you had to hire a full-time babysitter to look after Victoria while she convalesced after a bad bout of pneumonia. How are you going to meet those loan payments? How are you going to pay your rent? You were, I believe, fired this afternoon.'

The mocking glitter in his eyes told Courtenay better than any words that she had been right earlier when she'd guessed that he had been responsible for the loss of her job. Anger swelled inside her with such force that she thought she might burst a blood vessel. 'You *bastard*!' she cried. 'What right had you to pry into my affairs? And how did you manage to get Alf to fire me?'

'Ah, you've put two and two together.' His lips slanted in a cool smile. 'I'd hoped you might. It saves a lot of explanations——'

'It saves you nothing!' Courtenay spat out. 'I demand to know how you persuaded Alf to let me go.'

He shrugged his shoulders. 'I bought the company.'

'You bought the company?' Courtenay's voice was little more than a thready whisper. Dear God, did people really do things like that? She had thought they only happened in movies. . .had never really believed men like Graydon Winter existed. So, for once, Krystle had been right. Graydon Winter *was* the 'new man' at Mom's Own. 'But why?' she choked out. 'Surely not just because of me?'

'It was the only way. As soon as I realised Alf had a soft spot for you, I knew he'd never fire you of his own volition, no matter how much inducement I gave him. So——'

Courtenay interrupted wildly, 'So when you found out Mom's Own was on the edge of bankruptcy because Mr Ketterton couldn't afford to modernise the plant——'

'I bought him out. It was a good deal for Ketterton— he's now managing director, at a handsome salary. He has the security and benefits he didn't have before. . .and at his age it came as a blessing.' The lean features tilted in an artificially regretful expression as he went on, 'Then once I became owner, I realised the administrative staff was top-heavy, so I had to tell Alf to start down-sizing——'

'And of course you stipulated that I was to be the first sacrifice!' Courtenay exhaled a shivering breath. 'I've read about men like you—ruthless men, who trample on anyone and anything in their way—but you're the first I've ever met.' She shook her head. 'I feel sorry for you.'

'Oh, please don't.' His tone was mild. 'I always get what I want, one way or another. Perhaps you haven't learned yet, as I did a long time ago, that money is what makes the world go round. Money, Ms West, is power.'

'You *blackmailed* Alf! That was an unforgivable thing to do to such a nice——'

'He struggled a bit, I must admit, when I told him you had to go. . .but what choice did he have?'

'You are utterly despicable——'

'No, you're the one who's despicable.' He drained the last of his hot chocolate, and laid the mug on the counter-top. Then, hands thrust into the pockets of his cords, he walked around the table till he was only two feet from Courtenay. For a long moment he looked down at her, and the tension between them crackled like a brush fire in a heatwave. '"The Other Woman". . .' His voice was dangerously soft. 'It's not a pretty label, is it? But it's one that fits you to perfection. What is it about married men that appeals to you? Was my brother the first, or——'

'Hold it right there!' Courtenay stepped back a little. Though he hadn't touched her, she could feel her whole body tingle from his closeness. Forcing herself to concentrate on what she was saying, she went on, 'You don't have all the facts, Mr Winter. I was never—knowingly—the other woman. I had no idea your brother was married.'

'Just as you had no idea Alf Ketterton was married? Oh, come now, Ms West, do you really expect me to believe you? I know that Flo Ketterton has been a very good friend to you for several years, and yet you have no qualms about carrying on with her husband behind her back——'

'What you saw this afternoon you completely misinterpreted!'

'What I saw this afternoon was a vulnerable old man being sucked in by a shallow little bitch! Oh, I heard you. . .that silky-soft "I love you!" whispered in his ear as you kissed him. It made me sick! I'm going to take Victoria with me, to her family, where she belongs, before you taint her with your immorality——'

'How can I make you understand?' Her frustration made Courtenay feel as if her chest was going to explode. '*I didn't know Patrick had a wife*. In fact, I thought *I* was——'

She stopped abruptly. She had been about to say, I thought *I* was married to him myself. What was the use. . .what was the point in letting this man know just how stupid, how gullible she'd been? He would never believe her story anyway. And why would he? It was too bizarre. . .

'Oh, why go on?' she said flatly. 'You're not prepared to listen—and I really don't give a damn whether you believe anything I say or not. But I do give a damn about Vicky, and you will never take her from me—do you understand? *Never*!'

In the silence following her declaration, Courtenay heard Snoopy barking in the yard next door. Then, as the sound faded away, Graydon said harshly, 'Victoria is a Winter, and the Winters keep what belongs to them. I'm well aware that I have no legal claim to your child, but I'm not leaving her here. And if you refuse to let her go, then I shall have to take you along too——'

'Take me where?' Courtenay stared at him, eyes wide with disbelief.

'To my home in West Vancouver.'

'You're crazy!' She tried to calm her unsteady breathing. 'You really are. I'll give you two minutes to get out of here or I'm going to call the police!'

An angry shadow passed over his face, making his nose seem more aggressive, the lines grooving his cheeks more pronounced. 'Ms West, since my brother and his wife were killed my mother has been growing more listless by the day. I believe that meeting your daughter would be the key to her recovery. To have a grandchild has always been her dearest wish, and I plan to grant that wish. With or without your co-operation.'

Surely this couldn't be happening; surely she was trapped in some hideous nightmare? But even as Courtenay fought the hysteria threatening to bubble up inside her, she felt the onset of a trembling relief. Ever since she had seen Patrick's obituary, she had tried not to acknowledge the possibility that his family would somehow find out about her and try to take Vicky away. Well, Graydon Winter *had* found out about her—how, she couldn't even begin to guess—but though he had taken her job from her, and with his wealth and power could just as easily render her homeless, he could never take Vicky away from her. Why had she ever imagined he could? He had no leverage at all.

'I will never allow you to use my daughter,' she said, a shaky elation rising inside her as she tilted her chin defiantly. 'You may believe that money is power, but in this situation all the money in the world wouldn't change my mind. My child is not for sale!'

A shuffling sound in the hallway made her whirl round. Vicky was standing just inside the doorway, all the colour drained from her thin face. She was wearing her yellow T-shirt nightie, the one that said, 'Read me a Puppy Tale', and she had spilled hot chocolate down the front.

'Go back to your room.' Courtenay's voice shook. 'I'll be there shortly. Mr Winter is just leaving.'

She could see Vicky's lower lip trembling, but only for a moment, then her daughter's small white teeth bit down, and she shook her head, russet curls bouncing. Her bare feet were almost soundless on the lino as she came slowly into the room, her eyes fixed on the man watching her.

'I heard what you said.' Her voice was taut and controlled, reminding Courtenay of how she'd sounded earlier that afternoon when she had heard her uncle was in town. Reminding her of how she had sounded when she heard about Patrick's death. 'Uncle Graydon, I didn't mean to listen, I spilled my chocolate and I was on the way to the bathroom to sponge my nightie—when I heard you talking about my dad. I'm sorry, Mom, if I make you angry, but. . . I want. . . I want to. . .'

Courtenay couldn't speak. Emotion choked her as she stared at her daughter. Vicky had *never* defied her before!

'Yes, Victoria?' Graydon crossed the room in a couple of easy strides. He stopped in front of his niece, an encouraging expression on his face as he looked down at her. 'What were you going to say?'

Courtenay thought she knew her child. She was finding out with the power of a thunderbolt that she didn't know her at all. She watched numbly as Vicky pulled back her thin shoulders.

The bright blue eyes didn't meet Courtenay's as she said quietly, 'I want to meet my grandma.'

CHAPTER THREE

HARD December sunlight streamed through the net curtains in Courtenay's bedroom next morning as she packed her case. The snow outside gave the world a reflected brightness that contrasted harshly with her own dreary mood. How strange, she thought, that she had been strong enough to withstand Graydon Winter's ruthless will, only to be undone by the vulnerability of her child.

Dully she looked at the clothes spread out on the bed. They looked shabby and cheap.

Did she look shabby and cheap too? Reluctantly she raised her eyes to the mirror, but all she could see was the sheer exhaustion on her features. She was wearing her best sweater and her newest jeans for travelling, but even the soft pink angora next to her face did nothing to liven it. Her eyes looked more grey than green, her skin drawn tightly across her high cheekbones and straight nose.

'You look nice, Mom.'

The hesitant voice came from the doorway. Slowly Courtenay turned round. Vicky was ready to go. She'd been so good this morning, as if sensing that if she said one wrong word her mother would change her mind.

'So do you, honey.' Courtenay managed a smile. 'Would you go out to the gate and watch for the Mercedes?'

Moments later the back door banged and Courtenay could hear a child shouting something from the other side of the street, followed by Vicky's proudly yelled response, 'We're going to Vancouver to stay with my grandma over Christmas!'

Courtenay shivered. How could Vicky adjust so quickly to such a huge change in her life, walk—no, run—towards it with such effervescence, when she herself felt paralysed?

She had started packing an hour ago, but had kept finding herself sitting on the bed staring into space, not noticing how the time was passing. Quickly now she finished putting the clothes in her case, closed it, and took it through to the living-room.

Two weeks, that was what she'd agreed to; Vicky's Christmas vacation from school.

After Graydon had left, saying he'd pick them up at ten in the morning, Courtenay had lit the log, and she and Vicky had discussed what had happened while they drank their hot chocolate and wrapped their presents. Courtenay had gone to bed shortly after Vicky, but she couldn't sleep. She'd lain in the dark for hours, worrying.

She had always thought of Vicky and herself as a team, two against the world. It had been enough for her; she had assumed it was enough for her daughter too. Yet last night, Vicky had shown all too clearly that she was ready—no, eager!—to welcome a new uncle and grandmother into her life——

'He's here!' A jubilant shout shattered Courtenay's thoughts and made her heart give an apprehensive little flutter. The door burst open and Vicky erupted into the living-room. 'Do you want me to take your case out to the car?'

Courtenay nodded, and swallowed to ease the tightness of her throat. 'Thanks. Is yours outside?'

'Yup! Come on, Mom, we're waiting!'

Courtenay shrugged her shoulders into her jacket and, scooping up a pile of library books from the table, went out, locking the door behind her. When she turned the corner and saw Graydon standing by the Mercedes in his black leather jacket, her pulse gave an erratic leap. She had hoped that in the harsh light of day he would seem less attractive than he had the night before, but, with the glint of the sun emphasising the flinty blue-green of his eyes and the wind lifting his dark hair from his tanned brow, he looked even more devastatingly rugged than she had remembered.

He opened the front passenger door as she approached. 'Ready?' His voice was curt.

'And good morning to you too!' she retorted, her hair sliding back over her shoulders in a silky curtain as she flicked her head haughtily. 'What a lovely day for a drive.' She swept past him and, before he could have guessed what she was going to do, she had opened the back door and climbed in beside Vicky.

She heard him hiss something under his breath, and as she sank back against the luxurious upholstery the thought crossed her mind that it was probably quite a feat to have thwarted a man like Graydon Winter, even in this small way.

Allowing herself a wry smile, she watched him get into the driver's seat, watched him fling his jacket on to the passenger-seat. His sweater was slate-grey, and very expensive-looking. Alpaca, Courtenay decided. Would the wool feel as seductively soft as it looked, if she were to smooth her fingertips over his wide shoulders? Abruptly tightening her grip on the library books as she felt a little shiver run down her spine, she jerked her gaze away from him.

'Do you have to drop those off, Mom?'

'Oh. . .yes.' She leaned forward and said stiffly, 'Would you mind making a detour? I have to return some library books.'

Minutes later, given directions by Vicky, Graydon

stopped outside a small stuccoed building. Before
Courtenay could open her door, Graydon reached into
the back and swept the three books out of her hands.

'I'll take those.'

'Thanks.' Courtenay's response was grudging.

He paused to look at the titles, then read them aloud,
his tone growing increasingly incredulous. '*Origins of
Man, Time, Life and Man, Primate Evolution.*' His eyes met
Courtenay's in the mirror. 'Anthropology?' He raised
his eyebrows ironically.

'My mom's going to university one day!' Vicky
announced. 'It won't be for a long time, of course,
because she's going to wait till my education's finished,
but she studies every spare minute she has.'

When Graydon came back from the library, his
thoughts were obviously miles away. His brows were
gathered together, his eyes distant, as though he was
mulling over what he had just learned.

Courtenay wished Vicky hadn't said anything. She
wanted to keep at arm's length from Graydon Winter,
wanted to keep their relationship on a strictly imper-
sonal basis. . .yet within twenty-four hours he had discovered her secret dream.

And it seemed to be of interest to him.

Why?

Courtenay sat back and tried to relax, but found it
impossible. The ludicrous idea kept insinuating itself
into her head that Graydon Winter was for some reason
more interested in herself than he was in Vicky.

Which was foolish, because he hadn't even wanted to
take her to Vancouver; he had been forced to because
she had adamantly refused to let him take the child on
her own.

Not to mention the fact that the man obviously
despised her.

With a deep sigh, she looked out of the window, and

managed with a great effort to banish the ridiculous notion from her head.

They stopped for lunch around one o'clock at a roadside restaurant, and when they returned to the car Courtenay found herself being steered forcibly into the front passenger seat. Graydon produced a travelling rug for Vicky, who made herself comfortable with her *Pocket Encyclopaedia of Dogs*, and before they had gone five miles she was sound asleep.

Courtenay was intensely aware of the man sitting beside her. No one had ever made her feel the way he did—so tense and jumpy. It was as if his body was sending out invisible messages which were exciting her nerve-endings into tingling, vibrant life; she could almost feel them waving wildly in the air like antennae eagerly seeking contact. In addition, his aftershave was tantalising her nostrils; it had a musky outdoors fragrance that made her think of cool walks in the emerald-green of a cathedral forest——

'I want to talk to you before we get to Seacliffe House.'

His voice rasped into her treacherously straying thoughts. 'Seacliffe House?' she repeated confusedly.

'My home.'

'Oh.'

'It's about my mother. . . Alanna.' He tightened his grip on the steering wheel. 'Patrick and Beth were childhood sweethearts, and my mother used to boast that Paddy was the perfect husband——'

'Why are you telling me this?' Courtenay was no longer tense, jumpy, no longer under his sensual spell, her momentary weakness forgotten as anger and resentment took over. 'I don't give a *damn* what Patrick's relationship was with his wife——'

'Oh, I can well understand that!' Graydon's icy voice

hit her like a hard slap. 'I just want you to know the situation, so that you won't do or say anything to upset Alanna. I don't want her to think you and Paddy had an affair.'

'You're taking Vicky to meet your mother, but you want it kept a secret that Patrick and I were involved.' Sarcasm threaded Courtenay's voice. 'I'm *fascinated* to know just how you're going to explain Vicky's advent into the world. Do you intend telling your mother it was a virgin birth?'

'Hardly.' His tone was contemptuous. 'I doubt that even her unsuspecting mind would accept that. No, what I want you to do is tell her the truth. Not the story you told me last night, but what *really* happened. How you set out to seduce and trap my brother.'

Courtenay closed her eyes. Last night she had decided it would be useless trying to tell Graydon what had really happened. She had told herself he wouldn't listen. Perhaps she had made a mistake. Shouldn't she have at least given him the chance to hear what she had to say? Perhaps—bizarre though her story was—he might believe her. . .

'What really happened was that Patrick seduced me,' she said quietly, 'not the other way around.' It was an effort to keep her voice steady, but she knew that she had more chance of convincing him if she managed to appear calm. 'I didn't know he was married, and when he proposed to me after we'd known each other six weeks I accepted. We went through a marriage ceremony—a very private one—in a pretty little park at Whistler, and——'

Courtenay broke off with a startled cry as Graydon swerved on to the shoulder of the highway and slammed on the brakes. Vicky's book slid to the floor, and she murmured in her sleep before settling down again. As Graydon wrenched himself round in his seat and glared at Courtenay, she swallowed apprehensively. She had never in her life seen eyes burning with such fury.

'Get out!' he ordered harshly, and as she hesitated— wondering, disbelievingly, if he was going to abandon her here on this remote stretch of snow-packed high- way—he leaned across her and, twisting open her door- handle, shoved the door open. 'Unless you want your daughter to overhear what I'm going to say to you.'

No, she knew by the expression on his face that what he was going to say wasn't something Vicky should hear. Without replying, she got out and clicked the door shut quietly. Then, hunching into her jacket, she tugged up the zip as the icy wind threatened to tear the garment from her shoulders.

The snow crunched under Graydon's feet as he strode round the bonnet of the car and stopped in front of her, towering over her. He hadn't put on his leather jacket, and Courtenay found herself noticing—absurdly—that his sweater was exactly the same shade of grey as the sky.

'*A bigamist*?' Graydon's furious words seared her. 'You're accusing my brother of having committed a criminal act? Where's your proof?' he spat out scathingly. 'I'd really like to see it!'

Courtenay hugged her arms around her, wincing as her long hair was whipped across her face, stinging her eyes. 'I don't have proof——'

'Oh, my, my, my! What a surprise!'

'Let me finish! I don't have proof because it wasn't a real ceremony. It was all fake—though of course *I* didn't know it at the time. Patrick's so-called "marriage commissioner" was just a friend of his, and the witnesses were a couple of people he met in a coffee-shop. He told me——'

'Patrick told *me* you were a conniving little bitch,' Graydon's voice was swollen with anger, 'but even he couldn't have guessed you'd come up with such a wild story to whitewash yourself and your actions!'

'It's not a story! Oh, I don't understand why you can't bel——'

She broke off with a gasp as he grasped her shoulders, his hard fingers biting all the way through the thick pile of her jacket into her flesh. But despite her attempts to wriggle free she couldn't get away, and she shrank back from the menacing glitter in his eyes as he pulled her so close that his face was just two inches from hers.

'If you ever so much as whisper these accusations again,' he hissed, 'I'll take you to court and have you charged with slander, and I'll make sure you go to jail! My God, you must be out of your mind to think you can get away with spreading such lies! You little——'

Courtenay knew that whatever names he was calling her weren't complimentary; luckily they were drowned out as a massive oil tanker roared by on the highway, and all she could see was the vicious twist of his lips as he hurled the insults at her.

When he'd finished, he pushed her away abruptly, and Courtenay staggered back. She found herself clenching her fists, wishing with all her heart that she were a man so that she could punch that relentlessly determined jaw and knock him flying in the snow. Instead she concentrated all her efforts on calming the seething rage that was knotting her chest, and said in a strangled voice, 'It's a waste of time talking to you——'

'Well, at least you've got that straight!' he gritted.

'But that doesn't mean I can't talk to other people. I won't live a lie—I won't cover up for Patrick—he was a bastard!'

'I get the impression from the way Victoria talks about him that she doesn't share your opinion.'

'Of course she doesn't!' Courtenay glared up at him.

'I didn't want my daughter to know what her father was really like and grow up despising him—I felt it important that she should have a positive image of Patrick. In a perfect world every child would have two loving, caring parents. My child, through no fault of her own, was deprived of a father, but I've kept the truth about him to myself, and assured her he was a wonderful man. A man she would have loved. And she believes me.'

Graydon shoved back his thick black hair as the wind flattened it against his brow. 'She's a very sensitive little girl, isn't she?'

His voice was so soft, so lacking suddenly in hostility, that Courtenay felt a flicker of uncertainty. Was there, after all, a spark of compassion in this man?

'Yes,' she said warily. 'She's sensitive. . .and very vulnerable. I've been protective of her—perhaps too protective. But I've wanted to shield her from life's hurts as long as I can.'

'I can understand that. And I can see that the two of you have a close relationship.' A swirl of snowflakes swept past on the wind, and his black hair was all at once sprinkled with white. 'It would be a pity if something happened to. . .destroy that relationship.'

So he did have a softer side to him after all! Courtenay felt her defences slip, just a little. 'Don't worry,' she murmured. 'Nothing ever will.'

'Not even finding out that you hated her father?'

'But that won't happen. As I told you, I shall never tell her. . .' Courtenay's voice trailed away as she saw the subtle change in his expression. To her dismay, she saw that once again his eyes were glittering. . .but this time the hostility was edged with triumph. *Triumph*? Regarding what? As Courtenay's mind tried to come up with an answer, she felt the sour taste of bile rising in her throat. 'You wouldn't?' she whispered disbelievingly.

'Wouldn't I?' His tone was as biting as the winter wind. 'I want to bring Vicky to her grandmother, but at the same time I want the meeting to be as painless as possible for Alanna. And you are going to be instrumental in achieving that end.'

Courtenay turned away and gazed blindly at the snow-capped mountains sloping up from the highway. Patrick had used her. Now his brother also was determined to use her. Oh, in a different way, but still. . .he wanted to use her. She had sworn after she'd discovered the truth about Patrick that she'd never let any man use her again. She blinked away a sudden pricking of tears, and twisted round to look at Graydon again.

'If I refuse to co-operate,' she said raggedly, 'you'll turn Vicky against me.'

'It's your choice.' His eyes were cold. 'If you persist in telling your ridiculous lies, I promise you I'll repeat them word for word to your daughter. I think you'll see sense, though—and if you do Victoria's illusions will remain intact.'

Courtenay could feel herself start to shiver, and, hunching over a little, she cradled her arms round her waist. 'So,' she said shakily, 'you admit that what Vicky believes about Patrick is an illusion!'

His laugh was unpleasant. 'Oh, you've misunderstood. I meant. . . Victoria's illusions about *you* will remain intact. She won't find out what a lying little slut you are.'

Turning away from her with a gesture of arrogant dismissal, he opened the passenger door. A cry of angry protest rose to Courtenay's lips, but she choked it back. What good would it do to argue? She knew that for him the discussion was over.

Keeping her eyes averted from his grimly set face, she slid past him. As she did, she couldn't help but be aware of his musky male scent, and the warm fragrance of his breath as it brushed her cheek, and she felt her throat muscles tighten. What kind of a woman was she, that she could feel such a magnetic physical pull towards a man who was so monstrously unscrupulous? Tightening her lips, she sat down, and stared unseeingly out of the window as he got back into the car.

Once they were on the road again, he slid a cassette into the tape-deck. Bach. He'd obviously put on the music to give her time to think. But she didn't need any time, did she? She had no choice. What Graydon asked of her was that for two weeks she live a lie; the thought was unbearable. . .but the alternative—to have him destroy Vicky's trust in her—was even worse.

'All right.' She reached over and clicked off the music with an angry gesture. 'I'll go along with your deceit. But if there are lies to be told, you can tell them. *You* can tell your mother Patrick was a saint, for I can't. The words would stick in my craw. He was no saint; he was a selfish bastard—a manipulator. Just like you!'

It was dark when they reached Vancouver. Dark and wet. . .and the rush-hour.

Though it was Christmas Eve, Courtenay didn't feel even the smallest spark of excitement. Vicky, on the other hand, had been exclaiming with delight at the Christmas lights ever since they reached the city; now, as Graydon pulled off the busy street and into a crowded parking area, she piped up, 'Why are you stopping here?'

'Can't go to Grandma's without any presents, can we?'

For the first time since they had left Millar's Lake, Courtenay detected a lightening in his tone. She looked at him warily. 'Vicky and I have brought the presents we bought for each other,' she said thinly. 'I'm sorry, but my budget won't stretch to anything more.

Especially as I don't have a job to go back to,' she couldn't resist adding in an accusing tone.

'Let's get to the stores before they close.' He ignored her jibe. 'We'll talk about money later.'

Courtenay's further protests were arrogantly brushed aside, and she and Vicky were ushered out of the car and into the mall. As Vicky rushed on ahead, Courtenay found her arm grasped roughly.

'Don't argue in front of the child. I know damn well you don't have money to spend on luxuries. I'll foot the bill. I'll help you to choose a present for my mother, and one from Victoria too. We'll go in here. . .' He raised an arm and waved to Vicky, and she came running towards them, her face alight with wonder as Graydon led them through the doorway of an exclusive boutique.

'Buy whatever you like for your mother!' Courtenay snapped. 'I'm not here because I want to be. It's only because Vicky's happiness is so important to me that I agreed to come.'

With a toss of her hair, she walked away from him, and began looking at a display of fluffy shawls. As she fingered one she heard his voice behind her. 'Would you like one of those?'

'I thought it might be nice for your mother,' she retorted stiffly. 'They look so warm, yet the mohair is so light. . . Old people tend to feel the cold.'

Without looking at the price tag, Graydon selected two of the shawls, the butternut one Courtenay had been fingering and a turquoise one. Impatiently he turned to the assistant who was hovering beside him. 'Put these in a box, please, and wrap it in Christmas paper with a red satin bow.'

'Certainly, Mr Winter.'

As the young woman hurried to do his bidding, he glanced round with a frown, and his gaze fixed on a

black silk velvet cocktail dress draped on a mannequin
by the desk. To another, more mature assistant standing
close by, he said coolly, 'Please bring that dress for Ms
West to try on. And five or six of those in her size. . .'
He gestured towards several others on a rack by the
mannequin. 'I'll be back in ten minutes.'

Astonishment froze Courtenay for a moment, and by
the time she had gathered herself together sufficiently to
demand an explanation he was already several feet
away, Vicky's hand in his, and heading out of the shop.
She controlled an almost irresistible impulse to fling her
bag at his receding figure——

'This way, madam.' The silver-haired assistant was
as intimidating as she was elegant. Courtenay hesitated.
She had never been in a shop like this one before—she
usually bought her clothes through a mail-order cata-
logue—and suddenly she felt painfully aware of her
unsophisticated outfit. The assistant gestured towards
the dressing-room, a charm bracelet tinkling at her
wrist, her icy pink silk dress shimmering in the flores-
cent lighting.

Courtenay felt her palms become clammy. What was
she going to do? No way was she going to let Graydon
buy her a dress, but she certainly didn't want to go
scuttling ignominiously after him along the mall——

An impatient cough from the saleslady made up her
mind for her. 'I'm sorry,' she said quietly. 'I don't want
to try on the black dress.'

The woman frowned. 'But it's your size, I'm sure.'
Cool grey eyes swiftly assessed Courtenay's figure.
'You're a ten?'

'Yes, I am. It's just that I don't——'

'You don't like black?'

'I do. . .like black, I mean. And I think the dress is
beautiful. . .' Was she imagining it, or were all the other
salesladies staring at her? If only a deep hole would

appear in the middle of the rose-carpeted floor and swallow her up! 'It's just that I don't want to buy a new dress.'

The grey eyes opened wide. 'You're *sure*?'

'Yes, I'm quite sure.'

'Oh. Mr Winter did say he'd come back for you, though. If you wish, you can wait here in case you miss him—the mall's frightfully busy this evening.' She extended a slender hand towards an ornate pink and gold chair by a low table scattered with copies of *Vogue*. 'Do have a seat.' She glanced at the doorway. 'If you'll excuse me, I have another customer.'

Courtenay felt too restless to sit down. She paced back and forth between the display of shawls and the door, and became so engrossed in thoughts of what she'd like to do to the man who had put her in this embarrassing position that she didn't notice Vicky till she felt a tug on her sleeve.

'Uncle Graydon said he'd be back in a minute!' Her daughter's freckled face was alight with happiness and excitement. 'He bought me a dress, Mom!'

Courtenay bit back a protesting exclamation. It wouldn't do to let Vicky see how very angry Graydon had made her by his actions. And how could she disappoint her daughter now? With a supreme effort she counted to ten under her breath before she asked lightly, 'What colour, honey?'

'Pumpkin! He said my hair reminded him of a jack-o'-lantern! And Mom, my present for Grandma is a lace hankie, because Graydon says she doesn't like tissues. She doesn't believe in this modern age where everything's disposable. . .tissues and diapers and——'

'And marriages.' Graydon's low voice sounded in Courtenay's ear, making her jump. 'Which of the dresses did you choose?' he went on, taking out his wallet as Vicky skipped away towards the door.

Before Courtenay could reply, the silver-haired assist-ant came forward and interjected swiftly, 'Madam's colouring is perfect for the black velvet. And we have it in her size.' Fingering her pearls, she avoided meeting Courtenay's outraged glare.

'Did you like it?'

Courtenay dragged her furious gaze from the assistant and turned her attention to Graydon. His eyebrows were lifted in mocking question.

'It's lovely,' she announced tightly. 'But——' she moved her shoulders in what she hoped would pass for a bored shrug '—I've decided to take a raincheck. Perhaps I'll come back in January, when the sales are on. . . You know I have to watch my budget.'

She saw a dull flare of colour rise under Graydon's tanned cheeks. He looked as if he wanted to take her and shake her, but immediately he regained his self-control. Ignoring Courtenay, he addressed the woman behind the desk. 'I'll take the black. Thank you.' He tossed his credit card on the counter and turned his back on Courtenay.

As she stared at the broad shoulders in the expensive leather jacket, she felt an intense anger well up inside her. But what could she do, short of making a scene? Even if she did, she couldn't stop him purchasing the dress—but, she thought furiously, there was no way he could ever force her to wear it.

She stalked to the doorway to look for Vicky, and moments later Graydon emerged from the store laden with packages, his face like thunder. As the three of them made their way along the mall, Courtenay moved to take Vicky's hand, but Vicky didn't notice. The child skipped over to Graydon and hooked her arm into his, for all the world as if she'd forgotten her mother existed.

Courtenay couldn't have felt more jolted if Vicky had slapped her face.

* * *

Marine Drive, the main street which snaked its busy, narrow way through West Vancouver, was, to Courtenay, just a blur of lights and a nightmare of cars beyond the Mercedes's swishing windscreen wipers. But eventually the shopping district was left behind, and the road became quieter.

Courtenay saw the rain-lashed sign at the side of the road a second before Graydon turned off. *Seacliffe House.* Stone pillars marked the well-lit entrance, and when the Mercedes made a left turn and glided between them Courtenay felt her stomach begin to churn. What would Alanna be like. . .and how would she react to the situation that was about to be presented to her?

As Graydon drew the Mercedes to a halt by a wide flight of steps, for a moment Courtenay forgot all about the woman she was about to meet. She'd known the Winters were wealthy, but she had never imagined their home would look quite so spectacular. Even in the dark, and in the driving rain, she could see that it was like a castle—a modern castle, made of cedar, glass and rock. Its lines were sheer poetry, thrusting strongly skywards, repeating the line of the ancient pines rising majestically on either side of it.

Before she could catch her breath, she and Vicky were being ushered up the steps under the shelter of Graydon's enormous black umbrella; Courtenay had a fleeting impression of gigantic rhododendron bushes dripping with rain, and the strong tang of the ocean.

Then they were in a warm hallway, and Graydon was handing the umbrella to a woman of about thirty— obviously the housekeeper—who had appeared from nowhere as the front door closed behind them. She was tall and angular, with short brown hair and an energetic manner, and as she took their coats a friendly smile lit up her brown eyes.

'Your mother's in the drawing-room, Mr Winter.'

'Thanks, Livvy. Would you tell Wheeler to put the Mercedes in the garage, and ask him to bring in the cases and packages, please?'

Courtenay looked around in astonishment. She didn't know what she'd expected—perhaps wonderful marble floors, stunning designer furniture, a huge silver Christmas tree—but certainly not this! The hallway was bare, the carpet had been ripped up and the floorboards were showing, and the only furniture was what looked like a massive hallstand, shrouded in a white sheet. In one corner were pots of paint, brushes, rolls of wall-paper, and a stepladder.

Vicky looked up at her uncle. 'Are you going to paint the hall?'

Graydon put his arm on her shoulder and began guiding her across towards a door on the right, nodding to Courtenay to follow. 'Your grandma decided in June to have this part of the house redecorated. The workmen were organised to come in on schedule, but not long after they started Paddy. . .' he paused, and cleared his throat '. . .your father died. Your grandma didn't want workmen in the house. I'm afraid she still doesn't. Perhaps in the New Year she may change her mind. . .'

His eyes were hard as he looked at Courtenay and said in a low voice, 'Please remember, my mother has been through a lot. She can't stand up to any more unpleasant shocks. Whatever I say or do, go along with it.'

'I already promised you I would.' Courtenay's voice was cold. 'I'm not in the habit of going back on my word.'

He turned the doorknob and Courtenay felt Vicky's hand clutch hers. 'Mom, I'm scared.'

Courtenay almost said, So am I! but instead she squeezed Vicky's fingers reassuringly, and, whispering, 'Don't be, honey, it's going to be all right,' walked with her into the room.

CHAPTER FOUR

As GRAYDON closed the door behind them, Courtenay had a quick impression of dark glossy woods, artefacts of intricately carved stone, exotic Chinese lacquer screens, and chesterfields and armchairs covered richly with cream leather. A recessed bar was partially concealed by an ornamental tree, and a magnificent fireplace dominated the room, its dying embers glowing deep pink.

A small figure sat straight-backed in one of the huge armchairs, a magazine lying unopened on her lap. Motioning to Courtenay and Vicky to stay in the background, Graydon approached her.

'Mother. . .' He brushed a kiss on the pale cheek tilted up to him.

'So you're back.' His mother's smile was wistful. 'I was waiting for you. Worried about you. . .'

'I've told you before, you've no need to worry about me, Alanna.' He straightened and looked down at her. 'How have you been?'

'Fine, fine.' His mother lifted the magazine and leaned over to place it on a table by her side. 'Did you have a good trip?'

'Yes, a very. . .productive trip.' Graydon gestured to Courtenay and Vicky to join him. 'Mother, I have a surprise for you.'

Alanna must have sensed someone else's presence in the room, for, despite her son's protests, she got to her feet, leaning against him for support as she turned awkwardly. Eyes the same blue colour as Vicky's but a little faded encompassed the two strangers walking

towards her. Courtenay was intensely aware that
Graydon's gaze was fixed on her as she looked at the
woman who might have been her mother-in-law if things
had been different. Greying auburn hair, skin like
wrinkled rose petals, and a mouth—wide like Vicky's—
that was made for smiling, but was now down-tilted
wearily.

The faded eyes moved from Courtenay to Vicky and
back to Courtenay. . .and then, very slowly, back to
Vicky again. As Alanna stared at Vicky, the tension in
the air tightened till Courtenay felt as if she might
suffocate. She found herself struggling for breath as she
waited for the older woman to say something—anything!—but in the end it was Graydon whose words cut
into the taut silence.

'I've invited Courtenay and her daughter Victoria to
spend the holidays with us, Mother.' His tone was so
gentle that Courtenay could barely believe this was the
same man who had spoken so coldly to her just moments
before. He put his arms round his mother's shoulders,
and said, 'Sit down.'

'Let me look at the child.'

Courtenay felt as if every cell in her body had been
put on hold as she waited for Alanna's reaction. For a
long moment there was none, and then a pink flushed
patch appeared on each cheek.

'Aren't you going to say something?' Graydon tightened his supporting grip, and, for the first time,
Courtenay could see a muscle quiver in his jaw. He was
nervous too, she thought, and felt a faint flicker of
sympathy.

'We brought presents for you, Grandma.' Vicky
stepped forward, one hand out. 'I'm pleased to meet
you.'

Courtenay heard a sharp, indrawn hiss, and saw
Alanna's mouth work tremulously. She tried to imagine

the thoughts that would be running through the older woman's head as she looked at the little girl who had just announced that she was her grandchild.

After an endlessly long moment, Vicky's hand was clasped tightly. 'And I'm pleased to meet you too, child.'

'Mother, this is Courtenay West.'

Courtenay found herself being examined by a pair of bewildered, wary eyes. 'Mrs West.'

'It's Ms West, Mother,' Graydon said softly.

'Ms West.' Alanna's thin hand felt cold as it slid into Courtenay's. 'Gray told me he might be bringing someone home with him. . . I didn't realise it would be a woman—it's many years since he's brought one here.'

Dear lord. . . Courtenay felt a chill shiver down her spine—Alanna thought she and Graydon were involved! Would she also have concluded that Vicky was his child? She turned helplessly towards him.

'Let's all sit down,' he suggested, steering Alanna back to her chair. He motioned to Courtenay and Vicky to sit on the couch and he walked across to the bar. 'Sherry for you, Mother?' At Alanna's nod, he turned to Courtenay questioningly.

'Yes,' she murmured. 'Please.'

'And for you, Victoria, a little ginger ale?'

'Thank you.' Vicky was perched primly on the edge of her cushion, her eyes glued to her grandmother. For once in her life, Courtenay noted, she was mercifully silent.

Alanna waited till they all had their drinks in their hands before she spoke. 'Now, Graydon, start from the beginning and tell me how and where you and Courtenay met.'

Courtenay suddenly realised she was gripping the stem of the small crystal glass so tightly that she was in danger of snapping it. Taking a deep breath, she

loosened her grip. She had to stop him. . .she couldn't
sit by and let Vicky hear the lies he was going to tell
about her! Angrily she turned to him, but he met her
eyes with a look that ordered her to keep silent.

'First, let's have the fire stoked, Mother,' he suggested, and got up and pressed a bell set in the wall by
the fireplace.

Seconds later, the door opened and Livvy came in,
bearing an armful of logs. Excusing herself, she replen-
ished the fire. As she straightened, dusting her hands
together, she said, 'Was there something else, Mrs
Winter?'

'Is the room at the head of the stairs ready for guests?'

'Yes, Mrs Winter.'

'Then Ms West will sleep there, and Victoria can use
the room next door, with the adjoining bathroom.'

'Where's Blackie, Livvy?' Graydon bent to adjust one
of the logs.

'In the kitchen, Mr Winter.'

'Victoria. . .' he looked across at Vicky '. . .would you
like to go with Livvy? She'll introduce you to Blackie.'

'Who's Blackie?'

'He's my dog—a Lab——'

'A dog? You've got a dog? Oh, Uncle Graydon.'
Vicky's eyes were twin stars. 'Yes, I'd love to play with
him.'

Graydon smiled wryly. 'He'll be pleased to see you,
but he doesn't play much any more. He has arthritis
and is a very tired old fellow.'

His gaze met Courtenay's, and it was mocking. *Was
that subtle enough for you*? She could almost hear his
unspoken question. Automatically she nodded, barely
aware of what she was doing. Yes, he had manoeuvred
Vicky's removal from the room very subtly indeed.
When they had stopped for lunch, Vicky had taken her
Encyclopaedia of Dogs into the restaurant with her, and

during the course of the meal he had discovered that dogs were her passion.

'Is it OK if I go, Mom?'

'If it's all right with Mrs Winter.'

Alanna hesitated, obviously unwilling to have her newly discovered grandchild vanish so soon, but then she lifted a frail hand. 'Go, child—but don't be long.'

Vicky quickly finished her pop, and, setting the glass on the coffee-table, jumped to her feet. 'And after,' she addressed the housekeeper, 'will you please show me where your Christmas tree is? I want to put my mom's present under it.'

Livvy's glance swept anxiously to her employer before returning to Vicky. 'We don't have one this year.'

As the door closed behind them, on Vicky's murmur of disappointment, Courtenay noticed a frown settle on Alanna's brow. She felt a stab of compassion for her— Christmas trees had probably been the last thing on her mind as she faced up to the first Christmas Day without her younger son.

Graydon had moved to stand by the mantelpiece, one arm stretched along it. He cleared his throat. 'There's no doubt Victoria's a Winter, is there, Alanna? She's very like you, isn't she? She has your eyes, your hair, your smile. . .'

'It's a long time since I've had anything to smile about.' Alanna's voice was sad.

'Come now—it's Christmas Eve, and you've just had a wonderful surprise. You have a great deal to smile about! Mother, I don't quite know how to tell you how. . .this. . .all came about.' Graydon moved from his stance by the fire and came over to stand in front of Alanna. As he looked down at her, Courtenay could see the strain in his eyes.

Courtenay dragged her own gaze away and stared into the fire. Livvy had banked it with crisp alder logs, and flames were beginning to leap up the chimney like yellow tongues. The movement was hypnotic; she concentrated on it, trying to shut out Graydon's voice as he began talking to Alanna. His words were low and reassuring, and they seemed to Courtenay to be coming from very far away. It was as if she was emerging from an anaesthetic, and could hear, but not understand, what was being said around her. Oh, she couldn't shut it out completely—she desperately wished she could, for words and phrases drifted unerringly to her ears. . .

'Patrick. . .much   to   drink. . .   Courtenay. . .hotel . . .brief encounter. . .mistake. . .loved only Beth. . .'

A log slipped sideways, and a shower of sparks flittered up the chimney. The sound startled Courtenay from her trance, and she was aware that both Graydon and his mother were looking at her. Had they spoken to her? She didn't know, but she didn't want to wait to find out. She put down her glass and stood up, turning away her head, afraid they would see the tears glimmering in her eyes—but even more afraid of the dislike, the condemnation that would surely be in Alanna's expression.

'Excuse me,' she managed, 'I'm going upstairs.'

She heard Graydon say something just as she reached the door, but his words were a blur of sound with no meaning. She didn't want to hear him. She hated him. He was using her just as Patrick had used her. He was selfish, hard, arrogant. Her contempt for Patrick paled in comparison for what she felt for his brother. How in heaven's name had she ever let herself become involved with such a family?

By the time she reached the room at the head of the stairs, she was so blinded by her tears that she could hardly see.

*　*　*

Courtenay paced back and forth in the large bedroom with its queen-sized bed and beautiful grey stone fireplace. In the half-hour since she had come upstairs, she had tried without much success to contain the ugly emotions swirling inside her. Even the warm peach of the walls and plush carpet, and the graceful lines of the antique walnut bedroom suite, didn't have the calming effect they might have had in less trying circumstances.

When she heard the arrogant knock on the door she knew it was Graydon; she had been expecting him. She turned abruptly as he came in, and she compressed her lips as she saw the mocking expression on his darkly handsome face.

'Comfortable?' he asked.

Courtenay felt red daubs of colour stain her pale cheeks. 'I'll never be comfortable in this house. You've made sure of that.'

'Was there any option?' he enquired mildly, as he shrugged off his jacket and flung it on to the luxurious duvet that lay like a puffy silver-grey cloud on the bed. 'You've met Alanna—you've seen how frail she is. It was bad enough that she had to find out Patrick had betrayed Beth; if you'd added your trumped-up lies, I don't think she could have handled it.'

Frustration pounded through Courtenay's head, making it feel as if it was going to burst. 'It's a preposterous charade! If you'd told me before I left home that you were going to force it on me, I'd never have agreed to come. I *hate* lies! And especially this one. It puts me in an intolerable position! As long as you get your way, you don't give a tinker's damn what happens to anyone else.'

Graydon was wearing a shirt and tie under his sweater. With an impatient gesture, he suddenly tugged loose the knot of the tie, raising his chin and twisting his face to one side a little as he did so.

There was something about the line of his profile that caused Courtenay's throat muscles to tighten. She swallowed in an attempt to relax them again, and wondered confusedly what had caused the involuntary reaction. Was it the perfection of his rugged features. . .or was it that his gesture had been so essentially male? She turned away, pushing aside the disturbing questions as she walked to the window and stood with her back to him.

'You're quite wrong,' he said softly, 'about my not giving a damn how it'll affect anyone else. I would never do anything to hurt Victoria.'

The curtains hadn't been drawn, and Courtenay could see lights twinkling in the dark, across the inlet. She stared at them unseeingly, sighing as she thought about what Graydon had just said. Did he really care about Vicky? How could he? He had just met her! All the child was to him was a convenient tool, to use for his own ends.

She tensed as she heard him move up behind her.

'Can we try to be civil to each other?' he said. 'Children's antennae very quickly pick up on discordant vibes. For Victoria's sake, we should try to hide that we can't stand each other. Would you agree?'

So he was bringing it right out into the open, the antagonism that pulsed with almost frightening violence between them. But Courtenay knew he was right—it would spoil things for her daughter if she and Graydon were to be at each other's throats for the next two weeks.

'Yes,' she said coolly, 'I agree. It shouldn't be impossible, so long as we keep to neutral topics.' She stared at her reflection in the dark pane in front of her, and saw that her eyes held an unusually bright glitter. 'Topics such as. . .' she shrugged '. . .your house. It's very lovely.'

He was standing right at her back, so close that she could feel his breath gently lift a few strands of her hair.

And though she couldn't see him—only the outline of his reflection in the windowpane—she could feel his incredible magnetism tugging at her.

'Yes,' he said, 'we're fortunate. And Alanna has the gift of making a house a home. She's a nest-builder.'

Courtenay uttered a sound of protest as his hands gripped her shoulders and turned her round to face him. His fingers dug into her flesh like pincers as he went on, 'And this particular nest is big enough for all of us. For Alanna and myself. . .and you and Victoria. Permanently.'

Courtenay felt anger swell inside her—so much for keeping to neutral topics! 'It may well be large enough for four,' she snapped, tearing herself from his grip, 'and that may be what *you* want, but it's not what *I* want!'

'You could have a better life here.' Graydon shoved his hands arrogantly into his trouser pockets. 'You would have complete freedom to pursue your own career, have your own social life. They say there isn't room for two women in one kitchen—it would be simple to give you and Victoria your own self-contained suite here at Seacliffe. In time perhaps you and Alanna could become——'

'Friends?' Courtenay gave an incredulous laugh. '*Friends*? Is that what you were going to say? I should think you've already scuppered any chance of *that*!' She made no attempt to hide her resentment. 'But you're wasting your time, for I've no intention of moving down here. School reopens on January the seventh, and Vicky and I will be back in Millar's Lake by then.'

'Victoria's an extremely bright child—no one knows that better than you, I'm sure. She could be in a private school—there's a very good one just ten minutes away by car. She'd have every advantage. What are her special interests? Computers, drama, swimming? What I'm trying to say is——'

'What you're trying to *say* is, I can't give Vicky the material advantages you can; but what you're trying to *do* is take Vicky from me——'

'You're wrong.' Graydon's expression hardened. 'I just want what's best for her. She's a Winter, whether you like it or not, and nothing can change that. With Patrick gone, it seemed as if there'd be no more Winters, but now there's——'

'Now there's Vicky.' Courtenay felt fear creeping over her, but with a defiant tilt of her chin, she managed to say challengingly, 'Vicky isn't a Winter—she's a West. And if you're so concerned about the line dying out, there's a simple solution. Why don't you produce an heir yourself? I'm sure the women are lining up to warm your bed!'

Graydon turned away from her and pulled the cord to close the curtains. They swished across the glass in a blur of peach and grey silk. 'Unlike you,' he said softly, 'I don't believe in having children out of wedlock, and there's no woman on earth who could tempt me into marriage. Does that answer your question?'

Her anger emboldened her enough to taunt, 'So you can't be tempted into marriage? What's your problem, Graydon? Don't you like women? Perhaps you prefer——'

'Oh, I like women, make no mistake about that.' He lowered his black eyebrows grimly. 'Why the scornful smile? Are you trying to tell me you don't believe me?'

Before Courtenay could anticipate what he was going to do, he reached out and jerked her roughly against his wide muscled chest. 'Let me prove that you're wrong.'

Courtenay's breath was jolted out of her lungs with the impact, and involuntarily she reached for support. Her hands clutched his shoulders, and she found her fingers twisted in the very alpaca whose softness she'd speculated about in the Mercedes that morning.

She had never expected to be on touching terms with the luxurious sweater, but now that she was, she found its seductive silken quality was the last thing on her mind—all she could think of was the furious blue-green flare in Graydon's eyes. . .eyes that told her he was bent on only one thing.

With every ounce of energy in her body, she struggled to escape from him, wrenching her head to one side so forcibly that she felt pain slicing through her. But he twined his hands in her hair and forced her to face him again. For a fleeting second she had a swirling impression of dark hair, dilated pupils, and rugged features at frighteningly close range. . .and then with a small moan she screwed her eyes shut and braced herself for his brutal kiss.

The tremendous jolt of electricity that crackled between them when his lips met hers was something she should have anticipated but hadn't. It shafted through her, sizzling like lightning, and she wondered dizzily if her heart would stop.

Graydon stiffened, as if he too had been shocked by the powerful current. But only for a moment. Before Courtenay could gather her scattered senses, he had manoeuvred her beyond the window, forcing her backwards till she found herself pinned against the wall by her shoulders, like some fragile, captured butterfly.

Oh, how she despised him! But even as she searched for words strong enough to describe her feelings of contempt she realised despairingly that his sexual magnetism was like nothing she had ever experienced before. It skimmed over her skin like magic fingers, awakening senses she hadn't known existed. And his musky male scent, the unfamiliar texture of his tongue as he thrust it between her parted lips to tangle with her own, and the summer-sweet taste of him—all were more intoxicating than the finest champagne. She felt an excited tingling in her breasts, and somewhere low in her womb the beginning of a strange, coiling ache. . .

Slowly, inexorably, her defences weakened. A choking sound of despair came from her throat as she struggled to strengthen them. She mustn't give in to him—she mustn't!

But, even as she ordered herself to struggle, to her horror she found her hands sliding up over his broad shoulders, to his nape, and then to his thick, silky hair, where her slender fingers buried themselves. Dear lord, what was happening? Her mind was screaming, *Resist*! but every other cell in her body was whispering, *Surrender*. . .

A little gasp caught in her throat as she felt him slide his hands under her sweater—warm hands that moved smoothly over the silky nakedness of her back. Caressingly, in languorous circles, as if he was savouring the sensation of her skin against his own. She heard him give a smothered groan, and the erotic sound brought a swift influx of blood to her breasts, making them feel swollen.

As if he sensed her response, and wanted to release the creamy flesh, he began to fumble with the hook of her bra. Her body trembled, and her heartbeats began to drum urgently in her ears; involuntarily, her hips tilted forward. . .

And shock shuddered through her like an earthquake as she felt unmistakable evidence of his arousal.

He wanted her!

She jerked her head up and stared at him, her eyes wide with shock and dismay. This was something she had not anticipated.

He had set out to prove that he wasn't indifferent to the opposite sex, and he had certainly proved that—but in doing so he had revealed something that he surely hadn't wanted to reveal—he was vulnerable to her, physically.

Courtenay exhaled a shuddering breath, the sound echoed by his own. She saw his Adam's apple jerk convulsively, and then with a savage imprecation he threw her away from him, his face suddenly pale beneath the dark tan, anger glittering in eyes that were still glazed with desire.

As he walked to the bed, she became horribly aware that under her pink angora sweater her tingling nipples jutted like little pebbles. Biting her quivering lips, she folded her arms concealingly over her breasts.

It seemed like forever before he turned to face her, but it couldn't have been more than twenty or thirty seconds. When he did, his face was still pale, but his eyes had lost their glazed look and were once again clear and cold as a glacial lake.

'Does that prove my point?' There wasn't the slightest hint of unsteadiness in his voice.

'All it proves,' she said tightly, 'is that you're no gentleman.'

'Oh, I can be the perfect gentleman,' he parried with a contemptuous laugh, 'but only when I'm with a perfect lady.' He swept his jacket from the bed and slung it over one shoulder in a supremely self-assured gesture. 'And no lady would have reacted the way you did to a stranger's kiss. Especially a stranger she hated. You do *hate* me, don't you?'

'Yes, I hate you. As for your kiss. . .' She swallowed hard. 'Any woman would have reacted the way I did, unless she was made of stone. But you were aroused too,' she said quietly. 'You hate me, but you still want to make love to me. Take a long look at yourself, Graydon Winter. I really don't think you'll like what you see.'

Without waiting for his answer, she brushed past him

and walked swiftly to the bathroom, locking the door behind her.

Her body was shaking like a leaf as she leaned back against the wooden panels. He wanted her. . .they both knew that now.

But she wanted him too.

She would have to make sure she never gave him an opportunity to kiss her again, because she was putty in his hands.

And that could only lead to disaster.

CHAPTER FIVE

TENSION throbbed in the air with such intensity during dinner that Courtenay could have screamed.

When she had come downstairs, Alanna had greeted her with a distant 'Good evening', and turned away pointedly. Courtenay had felt a quick surge of resentment. What right did Patrick's mother have to judge her without first having asked to hear her side of the story? Had the other woman even paused to wonder if there *were* two sides?

In addition to her resentment, Courtenay had felt a rage that was almost frightening, and that rage was directed not at Alanna but at Graydon. He was the one who was responsible for this present situation. . .and though he was the one who had suggested they be civil to each other, his attitude threatened to make that impossible.

Fortunately Vicky was excited, and, as they ate, her eager voice prattled on about anything and everything in between mouthfuls of the delicious poached salmon dish which Livvy had served with baked potato, lightly steamed broccoli, and a fragrant, parsley-sprinkled sauce.

'Strawberries!' the child exclaimed when dessert was brought to the table. 'My favourite! We hardly ever have them—they're so expensive.'

'In winter they are.' Graydon glanced at his mother. 'Alanna?' He held out a small silver jug of cream, and as she nodded he passed it to her before turning his attention again to Vicky. 'But surely not in summer?'

'Not quite so expensive in summer.' Vicky popped a

69

juicy red berry into her mouth and chewed blissfully, swallowing before she answered. 'But they're still a treat because we have to watch how we spend our money. Mom and I have a special fund in the bank—it's for the orthodontist's bills—because my dentist says in two years I'm going to need braces for my buck teeth——'

'Overbite, honey,' Courtenay protested as she stiffly took the silver jug from Alanna and poured a little cream over Vicky's strawberries and then over her own. She was about to place the jug in the centre of the table when she realised that Graydon, who was sitting across from her, was holding his hand out to receive it.

His thumb caressed the tip of hers insolently as she passed it to him, and she felt a quiver of sensation dart through her at his touch. She snatched her hand away as if he'd burned it. Dear heaven, she had never met a man who could draw out such feelings of loathing in her! She wanted to lift her plate of strawberries and plant it right in his mocking face.

'Buck teeth, overbite. . .whatever!' Vicky shrugged her thin shoulders dismissingly. 'Anyway, when we go grocery shopping, Mom says, "Is this something we *need*, or just something we *want*?", then if the answer is we just want it, it's a treat. Most of the time, we make a sacrifice, and instead of buying the treat we put the money into our special fund.'

Alanna's eyebrows quirked, and her gaze moved briefly to Courtenay. Courtenay had expected to see the same cool indifference she'd been subjected to when she had come downstairs, but instead she saw a flicker of surprise—surprise mingled with approval? Before she could be sure, the shutters came down and Alanna turned back to Vicky. 'You're a very wise child for your years.'

'I am.' Vicky grinned at her. 'I heard Mr Ketterton say so to Mom one night when he came for supper when his wife was out of town.' She glanced at Courtenay for confirmation. 'Isn't that right, Mom?'

Courtenay glanced up, and found herself looking straight into Graydon's eyes—eyes which had become dark with contempt. What had she said or done to provoke it this time? she wondered. Somehow she managed to keep her tone light as she agreed, 'Yes, that's what he said, Vicky.'

'In case you're wondering, Mother,' Graydon tilted his chair back with a malicious smile, 'Mr Ketterton was Courtenay's boss. . . Oh, more than just her boss, he was also her. . .very good friend. . .'

Courtenay twisted her fingers together in her lap so tightly a shaft of pain shot up her arms. Oh, what an absolute bastard he was! He had made something innocent sound as if it had been. . .ugly. She'd only invited Alf to come for supper because she'd promised Flo she'd give him at least one good meal in her absence.

But before she could open her mouth to defend herself, Alanna pushed her chair from the table and got to her feet.

'I think we'll have our coffee in the drawing-room.' She turned her back on Courtenay as she spoke to her son. 'Will you ring for Livvy, dear?'

'Grandma, I'll go through to the kitchen and ask Livvy to bring the coffee.' Vicky got up and skipped across the room towards the door. 'I want to see Blackie.'

A vicious band of anger tightened around Courtenay's head as she walked across the hall a little behind Graydon and his mother. She didn't have to subject herself to this humiliating treatment—she would tell them she didn't want coffee, and go upstairs.

She took up a stance in the middle of the drawing-room, waiting for Graydon to help his mother into her armchair. He had taken off his sweater before dinner, and she could see his shoulder muscles and the muscles of his back rippling under his grey shirt. His trousers were tight-fitting, and she found her gaze drawn hypnotically over his taut buttocks and long muscled legs. His raw masculinity reached out to her like powerful tentacles. . .

A sigh of frustration escaped her. Why couldn't Patrick's brother have been an overweight, greasy old man, instead of a magnificent male animal with the compelling good looks of some matinee idol, and so much sex appeal that he could set her blood churning without even touching her?

As she stared at the thick black hair curling over the top of his shirt collar, she found herself remembering how it had felt beneath her fingertips—smooth, silk-textured and glossy. And other memories tumbled headlong into her mind, memories of the way her senses had responded to the moist thrust of his tongue, to the heated caress of his palms on her naked back. . .to the intimate pressure of his body against hers just before he had torn himself away. The erotic recollections stimulated a sudden tingling sensation in her nipples, a sensation that spread swiftly to every nerve-ending in her body, and, with an intensity that seemed to drain the blood from her veins, desire shuddered through her.

She drew in her breath in a soft little gasp, the sound so quiet she was sure no one could have heard it. . .but Graydon must have—or must have sensed it—for he straightened sharply.

Abruptly he turned towards her, a dark frown lowering his brow. Their eyes locked, and Courtenay saw his pupils dilate. Dismay brought a surge of colour to her cheeks. There was no mistaking the sudden awareness in his gaze as he looked at her. Awareness of how she was feeling. Awareness of her desire.

His eyes raked her body, but before she could read

their expression they became quickly hooded. 'Sit down,' he ordered, gesturing roughly towards the chesterfield.

Courtenay wanted to disobey, but her legs felt so wobbly that she knew if she tried to get to the stairs she would never make it across the hall. She moved unsteadily across the carpet and sank down on to the plush cushions, wishing she'd gone straight upstairs from the dining-room.

It was too late now. Miserably, she played with the hem of her sweater. How could she have lowered her guard to such an extent, letting him see how deeply he affected her.

'Would you care for a liqueur, Alanna?' His voice was even as he addressed his mother, as if he had already dismissed the highly charged exchange from his mind.

Before Alanna could respond, the door clicked open, and Livvy came in with a tray bearing a silver coffee service and bone china cups and saucers with an elegant gold-leaf pattern. She set it down on the table in front of the fire, and, acknowledging Alanna's murmured thanks, went out again.

Graydon had moved over to the bar. 'Mother?'

'No, thank you, dear.'

He looked enquiringly at Courtenay.

'I'll pass too, thanks.'

Alanna leaned forward and poured the coffee. 'Cream and sugar?' Her eyes slid briefly towards Courtenay.

'Black, please.'

As Graydon put Courtenay's coffee on the table in front of her, Alanna said, 'Gray, would you mind going up for my mints? They're in my bag—on the bedside table.'

'Are you feeling all right, Mother?' he queried.

'Just a little indigestion. Nothing to worry about.' She

smiled reassuringly up at him, and he nodded and walked across the room.

The moment the door was shut, Alanna's smile disappeared. Taking in a deep breath, she moved round in her chair so that she was facing Courtenay, and the enormous diamond and sapphire ring beside her wedding band sparkled as she grasped the arms of her wing chair determinedly.

'I wanted an opportunity to talk with you in private.' Her blue eyes were as hard as the sparkling gems in her ring. 'Graydon will be back in a moment, but no matter. What I have to say to you won't take long.'

Courtenay lifted her cup and saucer, noticing unhappily that her fingers were trembling. 'Yes, Mrs Winter?'

Alanna's voice rasped with dislike. 'Ms West, you are going to be in my home for the next two weeks. I think it would be best if we clear the air right at the start.'

Courtenay waited for her to go on. . .and hoped her blank expression gave away nothing of her rising anger.

'I'll be blunt.' Alanna's thin fingers curled more tightly over the padded arms of her chair. 'Graydon doesn't want you at Seacliffe House. . .and neither do I.'

Courtenay took a sip of her coffee and carefully placed the cup and saucer back on the table. 'You and Graydon have both made that quite clear to me,' she said tersely. 'I hope Graydon has made it just as clear to you that I didn't want to come here.'

Antagonism sparked from Alanna's eyes. 'I've always despised women who have affairs with married men——'

'And the married men who indulge in these affairs? How do you feel about them?' Courtenay flung back at her.

'I feel pity for them. Most of them are drawn into relationships without even knowing what's happening.

When they meet an attractive woman, one who's set her sights on them, they don't stand a chance. A woman like you can destroy so many lives. . .'

Courtenay stared into the fire through a red mist of anger—anger mixed with a pounding frustration. She couldn't go on like this, she just couldn't! Why had she ever promised Graydon she wouldn't contradict anything he said about her to his mother? He had, of course, vowed to destroy Vicky's trust in her if she broke that promise. . .but surely the relationship between herself and her daughter was strong enough to withstand any problems Graydon might hurl at it? Certainly she had told Vicky lies about Patrick—but those lies had been told only because she'd wanted to protect her. Surely Vicky would be able to understand that?

Courtenay swallowed. She was going to take the risk. She had to. She had to defend herself.

Drawing in a deep, shuddering breath, she raised her head, only to find the words she had planned to say dying in her throat.

She had caught the older woman off guard. Alanna was staring into space, and she had such an anguished expression in her faded blue eyes that Courtenay felt an ache of compassion. . .followed swiftly by a sharp stab of remorse. This was a grieving, hurting woman who needed to hear not the truth, but lies; needed to hear not angry words, but kind ones; needed to believe not that her son had been devious and callous, but an innocent who had been led astray. If Alanna was ever to learn what kind of a man Patrick had really been, there was no knowing how she would react. It might be too much for her to bear.

Courtenay straightened her shoulders as she made her decision. 'Mrs Winter. . .' Her voice was gentle. 'I'm sorry—about anything I may have done to make you unhappy. I truly didn't mean to upset you. And for the two weeks I'm here I'll try to keep out of your way.'

Alanna's eyelids flickered, and she turned her head round slowly. She looked slightly bewildered, but before she could respond the door opened and Graydon walked in.

He frowned, obviously sensing the tension in the room, and Courtenay saw accusation in his eyes as he sliced a narrowed gaze in her direction. Walking to his mother, he dropped her bag in her lap. 'There you are, Alanna. Now you can have your mint.'

The older woman slipped the strap over her wrist and struggled to her feet. 'Thank you, dear.' Her voice was shaky. 'But I needn't have bothered you after all—I think I'll go and lie down. The excitement has been too much for me. No, don't come up. . .' She held out her palm towards Graydon as he made to take her arm. 'I can manage.' Her 'Goodnight' was vague, her eyes perplexed as she let her gaze settle fleetingly on Courtenay as she passed her.

The moment the door closed behind his mother, Graydon turned on Courtenay, a muscle twitching angrily in his jaw.

'What the hell did you say to upset her?'

'I didn't say anything to upset her. On the contrary, I told her I'd try to keep out of her way while I'm here. And I intend to.' Courtenay picked up a copy of *Architectural Digest* from the coffee-table and began flipping over the pages, hoping he wouldn't notice her fingers were shaking.

He flung himself down on one of the armchairs, and out of the corner of her eye she could see him stretch out his long legs in front of him. In a little while she'd follow Alanna upstairs. She didn't want to take flight immediately—it would look as if she was going because of him. Which, of course, she was. . .but she didn't want him to know it. She couldn't risk staying here with him; already she felt the waves of electricity twanging between them.

For several minutes the only sound in the room was the rustle of paper as she flipped the pages of the magazine. Without really seeing them, she gazed at the glossy pictures—an Art Nouveau chair draped with a fuchsia silk gown, a portrait of Coco Chanel in her Paris apartment, an ad for Pheromone, 'the world's most precious perfume'——

'Christmas Eve.' Graydon's drawled words broke the silence, and she looked up to find that he had clasped his hands behind his head and was watching her from under his long black lashes. 'What would you and Victoria be doing if you were at home in Millar's Lake?'

So, Courtenay thought wryly, he was going to make an attempt to be civil after all! Well, no harm in co-operating; it could only make the situation less unpleasant. She glanced at her watch. 'I expect Vicky would be in bed by this time, and I would be——'

'And you would be entertaining one of your men friends? Perhaps. . . Alf?' The thin arrogant lips took on a cynical twist. 'Or do you have a whole fleet of married men just waiting in the wings for your call?'

Courtenay tossed the magazine furiously on to the coffee table and flung herself to her feet. So she'd been wrong—he'd had no *intention* of being civil!

Without responding to his taunt, she stalked out of the room, clicking the door shut sharply behind her.

Bastard! she fumed as she stomped off in search of Vicky. The man was an absolute bastard, and she detested him!

After Vicky was in bed, Courtenay soaked in a warm bath, but it did little to soothe her still raging anger. Once in bed, she switched off the light, hoping to fall asleep right away, but at midnight she was still awake. Not till around two-thirty did she begin to doze off. . .only to be disturbed by a muffled click that came from the corridor outside.

About five minutes later, she heard the faint creak of a mattress—it sounded as if it was right through the wall from her own. She swallowed. Vicky's room was on the other side from this one, and Alanna had gone to bed hours ago. Her neighbour could only be Graydon. And by the sound of it he was a mere few inches from her. . .

She heard the bed creak again as he shifted restlessly, and, with a fretful sigh, she twisted over on to her back, trying to make as little noise as possible. Was his mind in as much of a turmoil as her own? she wondered. Was his hatred of her so deep that he wouldn't be able to sleep either?

And despite that hatred, would he find the memory of their kiss intruding on his thoughts?

Would he find himself wondering—as she was—what would happen between them if the wall didn't exist?

Next morning, Courtenay was awakened by the sound of someone coming into her bedroom, and almost immediately her nostrils were assailed by the tantalising aroma of hot, strong coffee. With a sigh, she snuggled her face deeper into her pillows and tried to drift back to sleep again, wanting to recapture the dream shimmering at the outer edges of her consciousness.

Such a tantalising dream! Somehow the wall between the two bedrooms had dissolved, and Graydon was no longer in his own bed, but in hers. He had removed her pink nylon nightgown, the look in his eyes as he gazed on her uncovered body sending excitement quivering through her; and as he coaxed her to undress him all her inhibitions vanished. She felt wanton, and wild, and passionate, and she knew in her heart that when he took her, it would be in a ferment of ecstasy. She lay back on the puffy duvet, lips parted, body inflamed. He lowered himself over her and in a voice thick with emotion whispered——

'Your coffee, *madame*!'

The mocking words jarred Courtenay awake with harsh abruptness. Her eyelids flew open and as she looked up her throat tightened. The object of her fantasies was standing by her bed—not naked, as she'd been imagining him, but casually dressed in a disreputable petrol-blue cashmere sweater and a pair of even more disreputable jeans.

A tray was in his hands, and a sardonic light glittered in his eyes, as if—somehow—he knew she had been dreaming erotic dreams about him. 'Merry Christmas!'

Christmas Day—and she had slept in! Courtenay pushed herself up on one elbow, and as she tugged the sheet up to cover herself, was almost surprised to see that she was still wearing the pink nightie. With a sigh, she tried to clear the muzziness from her head. It was so confusing, the dream and the reality. Hard to distinguish between the two. How could she have surrendered so ecstatically to this man in her dreams, when she wanted to fight him every inch of the way when she was awake? Weaving her tousled blonde hair back from her face, she demanded, 'What are *you* doing here?'

Graydon laid the tray on her bedside table. 'I should have thought that was obvious. I've brought you a mug of coffee.' He turned away and walked to the window, where he swished open the curtains. It was a grey morning outside.

'I meant,' she said, 'why did *you* bring my coffee?'

'Because Livvy is busy in the kitchen.' He swivelled round, his thumbs tucked into his belt, his teeth gleaming white against his tanned skin as his lips curved in an arrogant smile. 'We have unexpected company. When you're ready, come downstairs and join the party.'

'What party?'

'The tree-trimming party.'

'I thought you didn't have a tree? Livvy said——'

'Alanna had a change of heart, and had a seven-foot pine delivered first thing this morning. Victoria and Bertie are decorating it now.'

'Bertie?'

'Family. . .friend,' he said abruptly. 'Do you want me to send Victoria up?'

For a moment Courtenay wondered why he had paused before he'd described Bertie as a friend. There had been an edge to his voice as he said the man's name. Odd. . .

With a shake of her head, she dismissed the subject, and turned her thoughts to her daughter. This was the first Christmas morning that Vicky hadn't bounced into Courtenay's room at dawn, insisting she come and open the presents. It hurt, but she was damned if she was going to let Graydon know it. 'No. . .' She managed a nonchalant gesture. 'That's all right. I'm sure she's having a good time.'

A nerve twitched at the base of his throat. 'I imagine she's used to amusing herself while you entertain male friends in your boudoir.'

Even as anger surged up inside her, Courtenay couldn't help noticing that his sweater was exactly the same colour as his eyes. The effect was devastating. She knew if she'd been standing her legs would have been weak as water. 'You're free to imagine whatever you want.' She levelled a hard gaze at him. 'Just don't think you're going to upset me any more with your unfounded accusations. I'm not going to listen to them.'

He moved restlessly to the foot of her bed and stood

there looking down at her. He obviously hadn't shaved—his jaw was darkly shadowed—and Courtenay felt her heartbeats quicken as she defiantly met his gaze. He was so very handsome. . .not in a sophisticated way, but in a very male and rugged way; he looked as if he'd be more comfortable in the jungle stalking tigers than standing in this elegantly furnished bedroom. Yet his eyes didn't give her the impression that he'd rather be anywhere other than where he was; in fact, the expression in their smoky depths telegraphed more clearly than he could possibly have known that where he wanted to be was in her bed. . .

As the realisation jolted into Courtenay's head, she felt her cheeks grow warm. In her dream, that was exactly where he *had* been!

Gritting her teeth, she jerked her mind from her dangerous thoughts. With an irritable twitch of her shoulders she leaned over towards the bedside table and grasped the handle of the coffee-mug, hardly aware that the sheet slipped almost to her waist as she did so.

What happened next, she wasn't sure—it all happened so fast. Did her elbow catch on the corner of her pillow? Did the heel of her hand hit the rim of the wooden tray? She had no time to wonder. One moment she had a firm grip of the mug, the next it had flown from her fingers and gone flying across the bed, sending a stinging stream of hot coffee over the swell of her breasts. She gave out a little yelp of dismay, and sat bolt upright, gasping as she tugged the soaking nightie from her skin.

Before she could blink, Graydon was at her side.

'Get up!' he barked, and as she sat, too numb with shock to move, he wrenched her from the bed and propelled her forcibly across the room and into the bathroom.

She stood shivering on the marble floor, able to do

nothing but watch as he grabbed a pink towel from the heated rail, and, holding it under the bath tap, swiftly saturated the thick terry cloth with icy cold water. But when he tried to tug the straps of her nightie over her shoulders and pull it off, she finally leapt into action.

'Stop!' she cried, snatching at his wrists. 'You don't have to——'

'This is no time for modesty,' he snapped. Tearing her fingers aside with rough impatience, he slid the flimsy garment down over her breasts to expose the already pink areas of burned skin.

'Damned fool!' His voice was gruff with anger. 'What the devil were you thinking about?'

Thinking of you, Courtenay thought hysterically. Thinking of the two of us in bed.

She shuddered as he tenderly wrapped the towel over her breasts, wincing as the icy fabric came in contact with the hot, stinging areas.

Even in her distress, she felt physically aware of him. He was so close as he wound the towel gently under her arms and round her back that if she'd moved her face four inches she could have brushed his charcoal-dark jaw with her lips. She could smell the musky fragrance from his hair, could hear his slightly unsteady breathing. As he carefully tucked the towel into place between her shoulderblades, she found herself watching him in the mirror. The backs of his tanned hands were sprinkled with crisp dark curls—really beautiful hands, she thought inconsequentially. The fingers were long and capable, and the spatulate nails bluntly cut.

There was something very reassuring about the competent way he was attending to her burns. He would have made a wonderful doctor, she acknowledged reluctantly—with his particular bedside manner, he was a natural. All his female patients would have fallen madly in love with him. Why, even she——

Courtenay drew in a shivering breath. Was she out of her *mind*, to be thinking such crazy thoughts? Next, she'd be imagining that she herself could fall in love with——

'There.' His abrupt voice broke into her wild musings. 'How does that feel now?'

'Oh. . .' Courtenay gathered her thoughts together with difficulty. 'A lot better.'

As their eyes met, she knew with absolute certainty that while he'd been tending to her he hadn't seen her as a woman, but just as someone who had been hurt, someone he wanted to help.

While she, on the other hand, had hardly been aware of the stinging pain, had instead been fantasising about having him as her doctor. . .a doctor she might even have fallen in love with. She had been so disturbingly aware of his physical attraction, of the magnetic pull of his body. . .

Was still only too aware of it. Panic surged through her as she realised that she hadn't shuttered her expression in time. It had given her away. She saw his pupils darken, felt her heart give an apprehensive lurch as an answering awareness sprang into the blue-green depths of his frowning gaze.

'How. . .how long must I keep this towel on?' She wanted to look away, but couldn't. It was as if he'd hypnotised her. 'I'm freezing!'

For a long moment Graydon didn't do or say anything, just stared at her as if she was a puzzle to which he didn't have the answer. Then, with an almost imperceptible shake of his head, he tugged his sweater off, revealing that he had been wearing nothing underneath. 'Here.' He spread the garment around her shoulders. 'That should help. I'd keep the towel in place for maybe five minutes or so, at least till you feel it's drained all the heat from your skin.'

'The coffee wasn't scalding hot—don't you think
you. . .over-reacted?' Courtenay couldn't drag her gaze
from his chest. It was darkly tanned, and thickly covered
with crisp jet black hair. Hair that also covered his
arms, and added to the intense male attraction of him.
She hugged herself and found herself running her palms
over the soft cashmere draped over her shoulders. The
scent of his body was on the garment; it plucked at her
senses, more potent than the most expensive, exotic
aphrodisiac.

'You don't want to take any risks,' he said curtly.
'Beauty as perfect as yours should be cherished.'

Courtenay's throat muscles tightened and she looked
up at him involuntarily. 'What a nice thing to say!' She
couldn't hide her surprise. 'But not true. I must look a
sight,' she glanced down with a shaky smile, 'with my
nightie hanging round my waist, a dripping wet towel
round my. . .top, no make-up, and my hair all mussed
from sleep——'

She broke off abruptly as he reached a hand out and
curled a finger round the damp hair hanging at her
shoulder. 'You *should* look a sight. . .' his voice was
husky '. . .but what you do look is damned appealing.'
His eyes were bewildered. 'How do you do it? How do
you manage to look so vulnerable and innocent?'

Considering the kind of woman you really are.

He didn't say the words, but he didn't have to; they
hung between them in the air anyway. Courtenay tried
to speak, to defend herself, but her throat muscles had
constricted even further. Why did it hurt so much that
he despised her? Till now it had only enraged her. What
was happening to her feelings for him? She stared up at
him, feeling lost and helpless.

His Adam's apple twitched convulsively, and in a
harsh tone, he went on, 'For heaven's sake, why do you

always look at me as if you're waiting for me to kiss you?'

Courtenay stared at him disbelievingly. Was that how she looked? She felt herself tremble. . .felt unable to meet his gaze any longer. . .and, dropping her eyes, found her attention drawn inexorably to his mouth.

It was a beautiful mouth, its firmness attesting to his authority, the sensual curve of the full lower lip suggesting an undeniably passionate nature. She felt her pulse-rate quicken as she recalled the seductive, velvety texture of his flesh on hers as he'd kissed her. . .

'You're mistaken,' she said raggedly, keeping her eyelids dipped so that her long lashes concealed her distress. 'Imagining things——'

'Am I?' His hands slid to her shoulders and she could feel them tremble as he held her. 'Look at me. . .' his voice had a tormented timbre '. . .and tell me I'm wrong.'

No, he wasn't wrong. She did want him to kiss her. She wanted it more than she'd ever wanted anything before.

Except, of course, for Vicky.

Vicky. She felt a cold chill ice her veins. She had almost forgotten about Vicky. The only thing—the only person—in the world that was important to her.

She must never lose sight of the fact that Graydon wanted to 'acquire' Vicky as a member of his family. And she knew enough about him already to be aware that when he wanted something he would stop at nothing till he got it. Look what he'd done already—bought out Mom's Own, just so that he could have her fired. It was despicable!

Would he stoop even lower to achieve his goal? Was he even now trying to ensnare her in some sexual trap with the intention of distracting her from her determination to keep herself and Vicky independent? If so, he had almost succeeded. . .

Thank heavens she had come to her senses in time!

With a supreme effort, she blanked all expression from her eyes before looking up at him. 'No,' she said, her voice absolutely steady, 'No, I don't want you to kiss me.' She forced herself not to flinch as his grip on her shoulders tightened. 'I don't know where on earth you got that idea. Now go—please!'

It seemed like forever before his hands dropped away.

'I'll send Livvy to your room with some ointment for those burns.' His voice was just as expressionless, just as steady as hers had been. 'And she can clean up.'

The air rustled around her as he walked to the bathroom door, and a moment later the bedroom door clicked shut.

Oh, dear lord. . .

Courtenay leaned back against the vanity unit. What was she going to do? It had been difficult enough to keep a wall between herself and this man when all she felt for him was physical attraction; but her hatred of him had helped. Now it was going to be more difficult. He had shown her a different side of himself as he'd tended to her burns, and a moment ago she had sensed a restless unhappiness in him. . .

She tugged at the nightie and it slid to the floor like a damp pink cloud. Wearily she stepped out of it, and, filling the sink with cold water, began rinsing the garment to remove the coffee stains. With a sigh, hardly aware that her hands were still plunged in the icy water, she leaned towards the mirror and stared into her eyes.

A little seed was growing inside her, a little seed of caring. Caring for this man she knew she should hate.

It was a seed that must never be allowed to flower.

CHAPTER SIX

THE aroma of roasting turkey wafted to Courtenay's nostrils as she came down the stairs fifteen minutes later. . .and the sound of female laughter drifted to her ears from the drawing-room. She hesitated on the bottom step, one hand resting on the banister. Graydon had mentioned someone called Bertie, but that merry tinkle hadn't come from a man. Had Bertie brought someone with him? A girlfriend? A wife?

Biting her lip uncertainly, she looked down at her belted lambswool dress. It was red, with a cowl neck and gathered skirt, and she knew it suited her. . .but it was three years old. Did it still look all right? Perhaps——

'Ah, there you are.'

She turned quickly as she heard Graydon's voice, and saw him striding towards her from the direction of the kitchen. He was once again wearing the old blue sweater, which she'd returned to him via Livvy, and she felt as if she were being dragged down into a warm, inescapable whirlpool as she felt the impact of his rugged male attraction.

His eyes darkened as he raked a swift gaze over her. 'That didn't take you long.' Irritably, he cleared a slight huskiness from his voice. 'How are your burns?'

'Oh. . .my skin still feels a little tender, but it doesn't look as inflamed as it did.'

'Good.'

He was so tall and powerfully built that as they walked towards the drawing-room together Courtenay felt as small and fragile as a piece of Dresden china! But a Dresden figurine had no feelings, whereas she had, and right now those feelings were in a turmoil—a turmoil caused by the tension throbbing between them. He couldn't be unaware of it, she thought helplessly.

'Mom!' As they entered the room, Vicky, in a pair of jeans and a rust-coloured sweater, hurled herself in their direction. 'Merry Christmas!'

Courtenay caught the jet-propelled rocket up in a bear-hug. 'Merry Christmas to you too, honey.'

She felt an enthusiastic kiss planted on her cheek, then Vicky wriggled free, scampering back to the perfectly shaped pine tree she was decorating in the far corner.

As Courtenay straightened, Graydon's hand firmly cupped her elbow and he ushered her towards the only other occupant of the room, a tall, willowy woman with a creamy complexion, a beauty spot on her left cheek, and a carefully casual tumble of wavy hair the colour of autumn bracken.

If this was Bertie's girlfriend, Courtenay thought wryly, he was making a big mistake leaving her with Graydon, for the woman's eyes—disturbingly clear cat-yellow eyes with feathery copper lashes and hard, pinpoint pupils—had latched on to him so hungrily that Courtenay felt embarrassed.

'Courtenay, this is Lady Atherton—Roberta.'

The other woman's upper lip curled almost imperceptibly as she scanned Courtenay. 'Call me Bertie, please! I dropped the "Lady" after Sir Alex—my husband— died. Now that I'm back in Canada, it seemed somehow. . .pretentious! I'm just plain Bertie Atherton.'

Courtenay felt her self-confidence slip a notch. She hadn't met a titled person before. . .and even though this woman now called herself 'plain Bertie Atherton', anyone less plain she had yet to see! Though her clothes were understated—knife-pleated wool skirt in creamy white, matching sweater, beautiful Italian leather pumps—she looked like one of the fabulous creatures Courtenay had seen gracing the pages of the *Architectural Digest* the night before.

'And you're Victoria's mother,' Bertie went on. 'You could have knocked me down with a feather.' She glanced at Vicky and lowered her voice. 'Of course, I can understand why the family isn't trying to keep it a secret. I've never seen a child more like her father.' She arched one arm towards Graydon in a graceful gesture that sent a hint of Joy wafting through the air. 'Alanna has the grandchild she's always longed for—I do think we should celebrate. How about some champagne, Graydon?'

'A wonderful idea.' He released Courtenay's elbow, and with a general 'Excuse me' turned and strode from the room.

Courtenay had felt trapped under his imprisoning grip, but immediately he released her she had a swift feeling of being stranded. Stranded with this intimidating fashion-plate! What on earth would they find to say to each other? But as Bertie slid her flat bottom on to the arm of one of the wing chairs by the fire, and crossed her legs elegantly, Vicky looked up from a container of fragile silver balls and said,

'Mom, Bertie used to live in London. She's actually had dinner with the Queen, and she's seen Lady Di's children, and oh, she's been to so many exciting places!'

Courtenay sighed gratefully as Vicky prattled on. She had forgotten that with a child around—and especially one as unselfconscious as Vicky—there were rarely any gaps in the conversation. Choosing a chair on the opposite side of the hearth from Bertie, she sat down and laced her fingers together in her lap.

Bertie waited till Vicky was busy hanging a ball to one of the lower branches of the tree, before leaning forward and saying to Courtenay in a soft voice, 'You and Patrick knew each other. . .way back when?' She flicked her gaze meaningfully in Vicky's direction, before fixing it on Courtenay again.

But Vicky had obviously been listening. Before her mother could answer, she piped up, 'Way back more than nine years ago! My tenth birthday is on the fifth of January!'

Bertie's eyes widened; she was obviously taken aback by the child's frankness.

Courtenay decided it would be a good idea to change the subject. 'Would you like to open your present now, honey?'

'Oh, no!' Vicky stood on tiptoe and hung a silver ball on one of the higher branches. 'At Seacliffe they always have their turkey around two, and open the presents after. That way, if there are candies, we can eat them without taking the edge off our appetite.' A bright flush tinged Vicky's cheeks. 'Isn't it a good idea?'

A good idea? Courtenay couldn't help thinking that if she'd suggested to Vicky in Millar's Lake that they should not open their presents first thing in the morning she'd have met with stiff resistance. So already Graydon was introducing Vicky to the traditions they held here, traditions different from the ones she and her daughter had always celebrated.

She hoped her resentment didn't show in her voice as she murmured, 'Mm. . .it's. . .*different*!'

Vicky clapped her hands. 'Oh, I almost forgot! Livvy said I could feed Blackie the bone Santa brought him! He's allowed his presents early!' She chuckled as she ran across the room, and slammed the door behind her as she left.

Courtenay stared into the fire. How quickly Vicky was adapting to her new surroundings. She herself was finding it much more difficult. . .

She looked up, to find that the exotic amber eyes that had stared at Graydon so greedily a few minutes ago were studying her from under lowered lashes.

'Graydon tells me,' Bertie drawled, 'that you and Victoria are to be staying at Seacliffe over the holidays.' Carelessly, the redhead played with an enormous topaz pendant dangling from her elegant neck. 'What a ghastly bore for him! There are so many parties at this time of year—I do hope your being here won't interfere with his social life.'

For a moment, Courtenay just stared at her, wondering if she had heard aright. Surely no one could be so rude! But the vindictive glint in the other woman's eyes only too clearly confirmed that she hadn't been mistaken.

Fury exploded inside Courtenay's chest like a great red flower. She'd had to contend with Graydon's hostility and she'd had to contend with Alanna's—did she now have to contend with this stranger's? Was the Winters' hostility going to extend to all their friends?

Well, she certainly didn't want to get into a slanging match with Roberta Atherton!

How she managed, she didn't know, but somehow she got to her feet. And as she met Bertie's maliciously glittering gaze, she managed to keep her trembling legs from sagging under her.

'Excuse me,' she said tightly, 'I'm going upstairs. Believe me, the very last thing I'd want to do would be to interfere with Graydon's social life!'

As she marched to the door, her footsteps were muffled by the thickness of the carpet; the only sound she could hear was her own harsh breathing. It took all the self-control she possessed not to scream. Bertie Atherton's insulting comments were the last straw. . .they really were!

She grasped the door-handle and snatched the door

open, almost colliding with Graydon, who was pushing it from the other side.

'Hey!' he protested, steadying the tray he was carrying, 'careful there! You almost made me drop——'

'Sorry.' Courtenay brushed past him without another word, her high heels clattering on the parquet floor as she half walked, half ran towards the bottom of the stairs.

She could sense him looking after her, but she didn't look back. He and Bertie Atherton—they deserved each other. She hoped they *choked* on their champagne!

By the time she reached the top of the stairs so absorbed was she in her anger that she had almost reached her bedroom door before she noticed Alanna coming towards her.

'Merry Christmas,' she choked out.

'Good morning.' The older woman's tone was stiff. 'Aren't you joining us for champagne?'

Afraid her voice might break if she tried to speak again, Courtenay dug her teeth tightly into her lower lip and shook her head. Standing aside to let Graydon's mother pass, she saw Alanna hesitate.

'You're not sick, are you? You look quite. . .pale.'

Afraid Alanna might see the telltale shine in her eyes, Courtenay averted her head and said in a muffled voice, 'I'm fine.'

Before Alanna could reply, Courtenay slipped into her room and closed the door. Breathing hard, she leaned back against it, her eyes closed. She could feel the tears try to escape from under her eyelids, and fiercely she squeezed them back. She was *not* going to cry, dammit! She was not going to let these people get to her.

Muscles tensed, she listened for Alanna's step on the stair, but it was quite some time before she heard it.

What had kept her? Why had she stood there, outside Courtenay's room? What had her thoughts been?

Courtenay pushed herself from the door, shaking her head. She was better not knowing what the other woman had been thinking about—it would certainly not have been complimentary to herself!

Moving to the window, Courtenay looked out through eyes that were slightly blurred, and noticed that a thick fog was rolling in from the ocean. Down below in the courtyard she could see Graydon's Mercedes, and alongside it a sporty ivory Jaguar. Did the second vehicle belong to Bertie?

And were Graydon and Bertie right at this moment discussing her in the drawing-room over a glass of champagne? Was he assuring Bertie that she could count on his appearance at all the parties he had promised to attend over the holidays? Was he also assuring the redhead that the only way he could get Vicky to Seacliffe was to bring Vicky's mother too?

Vicky!

Where *was* she?

Probably still with Blackie. Courtenay felt a sinking feeling of despair. No one wanted to be with her this Christmas morning—even her own daughter preferred to celebrate the occasion with a *dog*!

In the distance she suddenly heard the forlorn drone of a foghorn, and the sound seemed to accentuate her aching loneliness. A loneliness that seemed to numb her mind, a loneliness that made her feel listless, and unable to make an effort to move. . .

She was still standing slumped at the window fifteen minutes later when a movement in the courtyard caught her attention. Glancing down, she saw Bertie sweep across the gravel in a calf-length mink coat, escorted by Graydon. He opened the door of the Jaguar for her, and as he did she tilted her face up provocatively and said something.

Courtenay couldn't see his expression as he responded, but she did see him shake his head. Bertie grimaced, obviously not in agreement with whatever his response had been, and when he sliced the palm of his right hand in the air in a 'take-it-or-leave-it' gesture her chiselled lips compressed into a thin line of displeasure. For a long moment she stood frowning up at him, and then with an irritable shrug of her shoulders that made her mink swing open, she nodded. Stretching up on tiptoe, she moulded her sweatered figure against Graydon's, and, lacing her slender fingers around his neck to pull his head down, she kissed him full on the mouth.

Courtenay knew she should look away, but she couldn't. And she couldn't help wondering if the thick hair at Graydon's nape felt like silk to Bertie's touch as it had to hers, couldn't help wondering if his lips were sweet with the taste of champagne. . .

She shivered, wondering why there was such a sharp pain behind her breastbone. Bewildered, she ran the tip of her tongue over her upper lip. Why on earth was she feeling this way? She didn't care who Graydon was involved with. . .did she?

Though the kiss could have lasted only a few seconds, it seemed like forever to her. And she hadn't realised that she'd been holding her breath till she heard it hiss out as Bertie finally stepped away. The redhead turned up the collar of her mink, her mouth curved in a satisfied smile as she slipped into her car.

Graydon slammed the door—so hard that even through the double-glazed windows the sound cracked in Courtenay's ears—and as the Jaguar spat the gravel from under the rear wheels and shot away along the driveway he rammed his hands into the back pockets of his jeans and, spinning on his heel, turned towards the house.

The wind blowing the fog in from the ocean dishevelled his hair, and as he roughly raked the dark, flying strands into place he must have sensed someone watching him. Before Courtenay could anticipate what he was going to do, he jerked his head up and looked directly at her window.

Their eyes locked, and Courtenay froze. But only for a second. Before she could see his reaction, she hurriedly stepped back, frustration pounding through her head.

Damn! Why hadn't she stood her ground? She had been doing nothing wrong in looking out of the window, but by jumping back so guiltily she had acted as if she'd been caught doing something she was ashamed of. As if she'd been caught spying on them.

She sank down into a low upholstered chair, her cheeks hot with embarrassment, her eyes closed, and tried to shut out of her mind what had just happened.

But against the black backdrop of her eyelids she once again saw Bertie and Graydon kissing.

What was their relationship? she wondered restlessly. Were they lovers? Had she been witness to a lovers' tiff? What was it that Bertie had wanted of Graydon? Whatever it had been, he'd refused. . .and made a counter-offer, which Bertie had—reluctantly—accepted. Had they——?

With a sharp exclamation, Courtenay flung herself to her feet. Why was she wasting her time thinking about two people she didn't even like?

But as she paced back and forth in her room she had to admit to herself that she knew only too well why she was thinking about them—or, at any rate, thinking about Graydon. It was because, arrogant and manipulative though he might be, he intrigued her. He was the most attractive man she'd ever met, and she was beginning to find herself drawn to him.

Oh, not just physically—that had been there from the very beginning. But in other ways. When he'd treated her burns, he had shown her that he could be kind and gentle.

She wished now that he had kept that side of himself hidden from her. It would have been easier then to keep hating him.

When Courtenay went downstairs just before one, she found him alone in the drawing-room, sprawled in an armchair by the fire, an empty whisky glass in his hand. He had shaved and changed into a pair of silver-grey flannels and a crisp, icy blue shirt, and when he put down his glass and stood up to greet her with a sardonic smile Courtenay felt her stomach muscles clench. No man had a right to be so sexy-looking. . .

All through lunch, she was intensely aware of him. Vicky and Alanna became involved in a conversation about dogs, and though Graydon joined in from time to time she sensed that his remarks were just the remarks of a polite host. She hardly tasted the tender, perfectly browned turkey, or the flaky mince-pies and creamy ice-cream, so conscious was she of the narrowed blue-green eyes which seemed to be watching her every time she looked up. And afterwards, while coffee was served in the drawing-room and the presents were exchanged, it was only with a great effort that she managed, for Vicky's sake, to force a smile to her lips and pretend to be enjoying herself.

The last package to be opened was Alanna's, and it contained the mohair shawls.

The older woman murmured with surprise and pleasure as she removed the wrappings. 'Oh, aren't these lovely? Thank you, Gray, darling!'

'They're from Courtenay,' Graydon said tersely.

Courtenay's grip tightened on the paperback mystery Vicky had given her. 'No, Mrs Winter. . . Graydon bought them. I just chose them. . .'

'Put one on, Grandma—this one!' Vicky took the butternut shawl and draped it carefully over Alanna's thin shoulders. As she did, Alanna reached up and for a moment Courtenay thought she was going to snatch the scarf off and put it back in the box. But instead she just touched it and said rather stiltedly, 'I'm sure I'll find them very useful. Thank you.' Turning to Vicky, she went on, 'Now that I'm wearing my present, you must wear yours. Run upstairs and put on the new dress your uncle Graydon gave you.'

Vicky lifted the pretty pumpkin-coloured dress from the coffee-table and jumped to her feet. 'Come with me, Grandma!' Her voice was eager. 'The dress fastens down the back, and I won't be able to reach the buttons.'

Alanna's wide mouth turned up at the corners. 'All right, child.'

'Then will you teach me to play chess, Grandma?'

'Yes, I'd like that. There's a fire in my room, and a games table. That's where your grandad and I used to play.'

Courtenay slumped back in her chair as the door closed behind them. She had wanted to protest when Alanna had presented Vicky with an ivory chess set which had belonged to Patrick's father—it looked so expensive. But Vicky had been so thrilled with it that she had held her tongue.

What a strain it was, trying not to let Vicky sense the tension in the air. Thank goodness she and Alanna had gone upstairs! Now, if only Graydon would go away too. . .

But he didn't. He had risen from his chair as Alanna

rose from hers, and now he walked to the bar. Bending down beneath the counter, he took out a flat, rectangular parcel wrapped in silver with a scarlet bow.

He walked towards her and dropped it on to the coffee table in front of her.

'This is for you,' he said.

'What is it?'

'Open it and see.'

Courtenay shook her head. 'I don't want anything from you.' She stared unseeingly into the fire, vaguely hearing the sound of a phone in some other part of the house. It stopped after two rings.

'We've been invited to a New Year's Eve party at Bertie's waterfront condo in West Van.' The roughness of his tone drew her attention back to him, and she found him looking at her, his blue-green eyes hooded. 'It'll be a very glamorous affair. I don't imagine you've brought anything suitable to wear for such an occasion. Have you?'

Courtenay stared back at him numbly. 'A party? At *Bertie's*?' Why on earth would Bertie have invited her to a party after having intimated so coldly that morning that Courtenay had better not interfere in Graydon's social plans for the festive season——?

As she struggled to make sense of it, the scene she'd witnessed between Graydon and Bertie in the courtyard slithered into her mind, and she frowned. Was it possible that Bertie had been asking Graydon to her party. . .and that he'd refused to attend unless Courtenay was included in the invitation? But why would he have wanted her to——?

She blinked as she heard the rustle of paper, and realised that Graydon had ripped open the wrappings of the package. It was no surprise to her to see, nestled in pink tissue paper, the black velvet dress.

She gripped her hands together in her lap. 'I already told you,' she said tautly, 'I don't *want* that!'

Before he could reply, there was a sharp knock on the door, and as they both turned round Livvy came into the room with a worried expression on her face.

She stood just inside the doorway. 'Excuse me, Mr Winter.' She wiped her hands on her white apron. 'Nicholas Temple is on the phone. He said he's sorry to disturb you on Christmas Day, but he's just found out that *Ocean-West Two* has been involved in a collision in the harbour.'

'Oh, for heaven's sake!' Graydon's face darkened and Courtenay could see the muscles in his neck tighten. 'That damned fog!' A few curses rolled off his tongue, just under his breath, before he snapped, 'Tell Temple to go to the office and I'll meet him there in. . .' gold glinted at his wrist as he glanced brusquely at his watch '. . .fifteen minutes.'

'Yes, sir.' Livvy hurried away, leaving the door ajar.

Courtenay stood up. What was *Ocean-West Two*?

As if he read her thoughts, he said curtly, 'One of my tugs.'

'Do you *have* to go out?'

To her dismay, Courtenay heard a thread of disappointment in her voice. . .and as Graydon's hard glance sharpened she guessed he had heard it too. Oh, damn! 'Your mother,' she said breathlessly, in an effort to cover up, 'I was thinking of your mother. Won't she be upset that you're going out on Christmas afternoon? Surely a little tug can't be all that important?'

'You don't think I *want* to go out, do you?' Graydon shoved his black hair irritably back from his brow. 'But that "little tug" you so carelessly dismiss is worth close to four million dollars.'

Courtenay gulped. Four million dollars! She couldn't even begin to imagine that much money. The most she had ever had in her account was a thousand. . .and that was before Vicky had come down with pneumonia, and the resulting expenses had soon used all that up. . .and more!

She pushed herself from her chair and walked to the window. The fog had closed in and she could see nothing but the trees closest to the house. . .and of those the uppermost branches were shrouded in the dank grey blanket. What a dreary, dreary afternoon it was!

'I don't know how long I'll be.' Graydon's harsh voice penetrated her dismal thoughts. 'You'll be all right on your own?'

'Oh, yes,' she said with a mirthless laugh, 'I'll be all right on my own. I've learned to manage by myself very nicely, thank you. Your brother Patrick saw to *that*!'

The fire sparked and crackled at just that moment, drowning out his hissed retort, but she did hear him slam the drawing-room door as he left the room. In a couple of minutes she heard the front door slam shut too, the sound followed almost immediately by the roar of the Mercedes as he fired up the engine.

Courtenay could feel her heart thudding wildly against her ribcage. She shouldn't have sniped at him like that. . .not when he was already coping with bad news. Could they not even be in the same room without fighting? Why did they provoke such a fiercely charged response in each other? And why did she find that, after she'd stood up to him, instead of feeling good about her defiance she only felt more miserable?

Restlessly she walked over to the fire and sat down on the chesterfield. With a taut exclamation, she put the lid back on the box containing the black velvet dress and pushed the package to the far side of the coffee table. She would *never* wear that dress. And she would *never* go to a party at Bertie Atherton's!

* * *

Graydon didn't come home till very late.

Vicky and Alanna had gone to bed, Livvy had gone to a party, and after a relaxing bath Courtenay had decided to go downstairs and make herself some hot chocolate.

She was in the kitchen, stirring chocolate powder into a mug of scalded milk, when she heard the front door open.

Automatically she glanced down at her ancient pink robe and grimaced. Darn! Two more minutes and she'd have been back in her bedroom.

In her haste to put everything away, she knocked the lid of the chocolate tin on to the floor, where it rolled around noisily before coming to rest at the far end of the kitchen.

The rubber soles of her fluffy pink slippers scuffed on the tiled floor as she scurried over to pick it up, and she was just straightening, her cheeks flushed, when she heard Graydon's heavy tread in the doorway. She felt her breath catch in her throat.

'Oh, it's you,' he said, his tone flat. 'You're still up.'

'Mmm.' She darted the most fleeting of glances at him—just long enough to see that he had added a navy sweater to the blue shirt and grey flannels he'd had on earlier.

But even in that brief space of time his raw sexuality impacted on her like a blow to the solar plexus. Turning from him so that he wouldn't be able to see the bright colour that had flared in her cheeks, she busied herself rinsing the lid.

She heard him open the fridge, and from the corner of her eye she saw him take out the turkey carcase. Mug of hot chocolate in her hand, she was about to mutter 'Goodnight' and slip away, when, stealing another quick glance at him, she noticed with a jolt of concern that his face wore the grey tinge of utter exhaustion.

She hesitated, then said impulsively, 'You look as if you've had a rough night. The tug—is it badly damaged?'

He plucked the clingfilm wrap from the turkey and took a dinner plate from the cupboard, before uttering a clipped, 'Yes.'

'What happened?'

'A freighter rammed it in the fog.'

She waited for him to go on, but he didn't. Taking a knife from the drawer, he slashed several slices of meat from the breast, and tossed them abruptly on the plate before ramming the turkey back into the fridge.

'And?' she pressed.

He jerked his head round irritably. His eyes were weary, but as he took in her figure in the tightly belted robe she saw a spark of awareness flicker in the blue-green depths. . .a spark which was quickly hidden as he narrowed his gaze. 'And what?'

'There's surely more?' Courtenay tried to ignore the quivering sensation rippling through her. 'Was the other ship damaged? Whose fault was it? Was anyone hurt?'

He opened the bread bin and took out a bun. 'Why the hell would *you* want to know that?'

'Good grief, why wouldn't I want to know? You're the owner of a four-million-dollar tug which has just been damaged—it would be interesting to hear the details of how it happened.'

'You want to know what happened?' His tone was hard and challenging. . .and threaded with scepticism.

'Of course!'

'I find that hard to believe.'

'But why?' Courtenay couldn't hide her bewilderment. 'Wouldn't anyone?'

He laughed grimly. 'Not the kind of women I know.' Taking a ripe tomato from a basket on the counter-top, he sliced it and put it inside the bun, along with the turkey. After liberally sprinkling it with pepper, he closed the bun and cut it in two. 'The kind of women I know aren't interested in the nuts and bolts of how I make my money. They're just interested in the money.'

'You must know the wrong kind of women,' Courtenay said steadily.

'Maybe I do at that,' he muttered, his words barely audible.

'So. . .are you going to tell me what happened?'

His lips took on a mocking twist. 'You really want to know?'

'Yes, I really want to know.'

'All right. Be ready at seven tomorrow morning and I'll take you down to the dry-dock. You can see for yourself exactly what happened.'

Courtenay could tell by his expression that he expected her to come up with some excuse and refuse; she could tell he'd thought her interest was faked, and had decided to call her bluff. Well, he was wrong.

Recklessly, she retorted, 'Fine. I'll be ready.'

She could see she'd taken him aback. Indecision shadowed his features briefly, then the wide shoulders lifted in a shrug.

He opened the fridge again and took out a can of beer. Snapping it open, he drank from it thirstily. Then, wiping the froth from his lips, he growled, 'Wear something warm.'

'I will.' Courtenay hesitated for a moment. 'I'll see you in the morning, then?'

Graydon placed his plate on the table, and, scraping back one of the chairs, sat down, can of beer in his hand.

'Goodnight,' he said.

Clutching her hot chocolate, Courtenay left the kitchen and made for the stairs, her mind whirling in confusion. Why had she insisted on going with him to see the tug? Hadn't she decided to keep as much distance between herself and Graydon as possible?

This man was the enemy. . .wasn't he?

She felt a sinking feeling of despair when she realised she didn't know the answers to her own questions.

CHAPTER SEVEN

A RAW wind whipped Courtenay's hair around her face as she and Graydon walked from the Ocean-West Shipyards car park to the entrance gate next morning. Shivering, she tugged up the zip of her ski jacket, absently noticing the pungent aroma of woodchips and oil in the tangy ocean air.

'Mornin', Mr Winter.' The watchman's whiskered face creased in a grin. 'You're bright and early today!' He cast an appreciative glance at Courtenay. 'Mornin', miss.'

He opened the high chain-link gate to let them in, and as it creaked noisily behind them a grey-speckled seagull wheeled upwards from atop a nearby garbage can, screaming in outrage at being disturbed.

Courtenay hurried to catch up with Graydon's long stride. Like her own, his hair was dishevelled by the wind, and, with his wide shoulders encased in his black leather jacket, and his long, muscled legs snug in tight-fitting black jeans, he presented a picture so devastatingly male that she felt a myriad restless sexual urgings spring to life inside her—urgings that set her pulses racing and drew the very air from her lungs.

'Not many people around.' She hoped he would put her breathlessness down to her hurried pace.

'Skeleton staff today, because of the holiday.'

'Mmm.' Courtenay glanced up sideways, and as her gaze took in the perfection of his rugged profile she felt herself almost stunned by the sheer male beauty of him.

What was happening to her? she wondered bewilderedly. Graydon Winter's was not the first perfect profile she'd seen in her twenty-seven years. . .so why did it fascinate her so? Why did she feel such a longing to trace a fingertip over the strong line of the brow, the nose, the jaw. . .the perfectly moulded lips? Surely these were the yearnings of a love-struck teenager. . .

She dragged her gaze away, and with an effort focused her attention on the massive yellow cranes rearing grotesquely overhead, and the weatherbeaten grey buildings towering on either side of her.

'Through here.' Graydon grasped her arm and led her along a path between two of the buildings, and moments later they came out on the other side. Across the harbour Courtenay could see the lights of Vancouver twinkling in the purple-grey of the early morning, and, straight ahead, less than ten yards away, was the dry dock. In it was the towboat, a sturdy vessel with the Ocean-West logo—a huge white 'OW'—on its black funnel.

Graydon's grip tightened briefly as they moved close to the edge of the deep yawning chasm, then he released her. 'There it is.' His tone was wry. 'The *Ocean-West Two*. Or what's left of it.'

Courtenay shook her head in disbelief. 'I hadn't expected the damage to be quite so bad.' Her wide-eyed gaze encompassed the enormous hole in the bow under the waterline, the steel plate ripped jaggedly open, revealing the interior of the vessel. After a long moment, she turned and looked up at him. 'I really would like to know what happened. Will you tell me. . .now?'

His eyes were narrowed as he ran an assessing gaze over the towboat. 'She was tied up in Centennial Dock when a freighter making for another dock lost its bearings in the fog and bore down on her. Preliminary reports indicate that it was pilot error.'

'But you're insured?'

'Of course. I expect to be heavily involved with insurance litigation over damages.'

'Was anyone hurt?'

'No.' Graydon shoved back flying strands of his black hair with an impatient gesture. 'At least we have that to be thankful for.'

They stood in silence for a while, then as a fierce gust of wind blew dust up into Courtenay's face she grimaced and turned away from the dry dock.

'Thanks for taking me down here,' she said. 'I've never seen anything like this before.'

Flicking up the collar of her jacket, she wandered towards the edge of the harbour. Peering down, she saw that the water below was inky black, with shafts of light from an overhead lamp darting and glimmering on its rippled surface.

Inhaling deeply, she looked up at Graydon with an impulsive smile. 'I love the smell of the ocean. I come from a long line of Scottish fishermen on my mother's side—and they were descended from the Vikings!—so the sea's probably in my blood.'

He jammed his hands in his pockets and rested his foot on a bollard. 'Is your mother still alive?'

Courtenay sensed that the question hadn't come easily to him; he probably found it difficult to carry on a normal conversation with her, in view of the conflict between them.

'She died when I was two. My father brought me up.' Despite her attempt to sound casual, Courtenay didn't quite manage to keep the bitterness from her tone. 'He married again when I was fourteen.'

'How do you get along with your stepmother?'

Courtenay shrugged. '*They* get along well together. Isn't that all that matters?'

There was a brief pause before he said, 'And Victoria—does she like them?'

'She hasn't ever met them.'

'Why on earth not?' There was no mistaking the accusation in his voice.

'Because they—like you—didn't believe me when I told them Patrick had tricked me into a sham marriage,' Courtenay snapped. Before he could say anything, she went on determinedly, 'I moved from Whistler back to Kelowna, my home town, when I was eight months pregnant. I knew my savings would run out soon after the baby was born, so I went to my father—swallowed my pride and asked him for a loan to tide me over. He told me to get out—said I'd made my bed and I would have to lie in it.'

'How in hell's name did you manage?' The words erupted spontaneously from Graydon's lips.

'I had to go on welfare.'

Face bleak as she recalled those dreadful days when she'd had barely enough money on which to scrape by, Courtenay began walking slowly along the wharf, Graydon's heavy step echoing the sharper sound of her high-heeled boots as he moved along with her.

'I got subsidised day-care and rent,' she went on, 'and applied for a student loan so I could take a secretarial course. By the time I graduated, Vicky was two. I wanted to make a fresh start, so we moved to Millar's Lake——'

'And that's where you met Alf.'

His back was to the light, his face in shadow so that she couldn't see his expression, but she could hear the contempt edging his tone.

'He gave me a job, when jobs were very hard to come by.' Courtenay's fingers curled into fists at her sides. 'You're absolutely wrong in thinking there was anything between the two of us. Not many people know that he and Flo had a daughter, Dawn, who died of leukaemia when she was four. They've told me many times in the past few years that Vicky and I have helped fill an empty place in their hearts. Go on misjudging me if you want, but you *mustn't* go on thinking badly of Alf. He doesn't deserve it. Can't you believe me?' Her features were twisted with distress as she looked up at him.

'It's hard not to,' he said, faintly mocking, 'when you appeal to me with those beautiful sea-green eyes. You're very convincing. But if I were to believe you about Alf, then——'

'Then you'd have to wonder if you'd been wrong about what happened between Patrick and me too,' Courtenay's tone hardened, 'and I can tell that there's no chance of your changing your mind about that.'

'Why should I believe *you*, over my own brother?'

Despite her down-filled jacket, Courtenay felt herself begin to shiver. She stopped walking, and hugging her arms around herself, met his challenging gaze. 'Because I'm telling the truth. And besides, if you believed me——'

She broke off abruptly, appalled by what she had been about to say: if you believed what I told you then you wouldn't have any reason to hate me. Horror spilled through her; was that what she wanted? For him not to hate her? She shuddered. When had that happened. . .?

'If I believed you. . .then what?' His demanding voice scraped across her nerve-endings.

Courtenay looked up at him numbly. How could she tell him what she'd been thinking? She felt her teeth begin to chatter as she floundered in her confusion. Even if she'd known what to say, she doubted if she could have spoken.

He frowned. 'You're frozen.' Grasping her elbow, he swung her away from the harbour's edge, saying, 'I have to go to my office to pick up some notes. I'll put on a pot of coffee and get you warmed up. . .'

It was obvious he had dismissed their conversation

from his mind. If only she could do so as easily, Courtenay thought miserably. But by the time they reached the office, a modern, three-storey building a few minutes' walk from the dry dock, she felt more in control of herself again. Still, she was thankful they met no one as they made their way across the foyer and along a tiled corridor to a room at the far end.

'This is it.' Graydon unlocked the door and ushered her in.

The room was in darkness, and in the split second before he switched on the light Courtenay could see that the far wall was windowed and looked out across the harbour to the city. Dawn was just beginning to break, and fingers of pink were crawling over the high-rise office buildings.

Graydon shrugged off his leather jacket, revealing his grey alpaca sweater worn over a casual open-necked shirt with a small grey and white check. He moved towards Courtenay. 'Let me have your jacket.'

His fingertips brushed the sensitive skin at her nape as he slid the garment from her shoulders, and as electricity sizzled through her she almost jumped. Her throat tightened at his closeness, at the now familiar male scent of his body, and she moved back from him.

Frowning, he threw the jacket on top of his own and crossed to a door leading to a modern kitchen area. 'Make yourself at home,' he said brusquely. 'I'll put on the coffee.'

Courtenay looked around curiously. The office was furnished in a rugged, masculine way, with a massive oak desk, and slate-blue leather furniture grouped around a low coffee-table by the window. Magnificent oil seascapes graced one wall, and she stood admiring them for several minutes before crossing to sit on Graydon's swivel chair.

She let her gaze wander over his desk. His computer

was a state-of-the-art IBM, hooked up to a sleek printer, and alongside it was a pile of files. Next to his in-basket was a flourishing poinsettia plant, with a small card daintily nestled among its large scarlet floral leaves. Idly, Courtenay extricated the card, and glanced at its inscribed message.

'Enjoy! All my love, darling. Bertie.'

Courtenay felt her heart constrict, just a little, and just for a moment. Not wanting to analyse her reaction, she ignored it, and, curling her upper lip, she sniffed disdainfully. Those two were made for each other! They had so much in common. Both were rich, hard, selfish, manipulative. . .

As she tossed the card back among the leaves, she heard a sound behind her, and, looking up, she found Graydon at her shoulder, two mugs of steaming coffee in his hands.

'Snooping?' He cocked a mocking eyebrow down at her.

'Caught in the act!' she retorted with a faint smile. 'What's my punishment to be?'

She felt her throat muscles tighten as she took one of the mugs from him. There was no mistaking the twinkle of amusement in his eyes. . .and for the first time those unusual eyes seemed to be more green than blue, a disconcertingly warm green that seemed to wrap itself around her heart.

'I'm not sure,' he murmured slowly, 'but I'll come up with something. Trust me.'

He was holding his mug level with his chest and the steam rose from his coffee, so that he was looking through it. When it dissipated, his eyes were once again inscrutable, and Courtenay wondered if she had just imagined the intimacy of the moment.

She watched warily as he moved across to the window; watched as he set his mug on the low table and sprawled back lazily on the chesterfield. 'So,' he said, 'what do you think of my office?'

Courtenay took a sip from the strong hot brew. 'Mmm, you make a good cup of coffee. The office? I think it's beautiful. It must be a joy to come to a place like this every day.'

'I hoped that would be your answer. Tell me. . .' he crossed his right leg casually over his left knee '. . .how would you like to work here?'

Without giving her time to assimilate his proposal, he went on silkily, 'My secretary's about to retire and I'm looking for a replacement. You'd make a helluva lot more money than you'd make up in Millar's Lake, and if you took the job you could move down to Vancouver and stay at Seacliffe and *still* keep your damned independence!'

Courtenay gritted her teeth. She just couldn't let herself relax for one *minute* while he was around; under that smooth surface, his mind must be perpetually whirling round, searching for ways to keep her—and therefore Vicky—in his clutches.

'That's very generous of you,' she answered stiffly. 'Thanks. . .but no, thanks.'

'Think it over,' he persisted. 'It can be a mistake to turn down an offer without——'

'I don't need to think it over!' she said forcefully. 'My mind is made up.'

Graydon Winter was not a man, Courtenay decided, who easily took 'no' for an answer. She could tell by the grim set of his jaw that her firm refusal had angered him, could tell by the way he unconsciously flexed his shoulder muscles that he longed to take her and shake her into submission. How very galling it must be for him to be thwarted, when he was used to getting his own way! But she knew he wouldn't give up without a fight. Though there was no sound in the room as she concentrated on finishing her coffee; she could have sworn she heard the clash of steel against steel, sword against shield, as she tensed herself against the incredible force of his will.

No sooner had she drained the last drop from her mug than he stood up. 'Ready?' he said tersely.

'Yes.' Her response was clipped.

Her pink angora sweater had ridden up a little while she was sitting, and as she got to her feet she tugged it down over her hips, smoothing it with her palms before she lifted her mug. As she straightened, she chanced to glance at Graydon and saw to her dismay that his gaze was fixed on her breasts, their full contours no doubt revealed by the clinging fabric of her sweater. She made an involuntary little sound, and their eyes met. The awareness springing to life in his set her pulses racing.

Damn! Courtenay spun on her heel and hurried to the kitchen. The sexual tension that had been pulling loosely between them all morning had snapped suddenly and alarmingly to vibrant, electric life. She wanted to run, but she was trapped. She should have made for the door, not the kitchen! Her heart leaped against her throat as she heard Graydon come up behind her.

Fingers shaking, she rinsed her mug under the tap. Then, leaving it on the draining rack, she turned, and choked back a gasp as she almost bumped into him. He was much closer than she had expected. So close that she could smell the coffee fragrance on his breath, and see the beads of sweat coating his upper lip. His mouth looked more sensually soft than she'd ever seen it. It was almost impossible for her to look away, but with a supreme effort she lifted her gaze to his eyes. A mistake. They were smouldering with barely concealed desire, their heat drawing her like the blue-green flame of a winter fire.

She made to side-step him. 'Excuse me,' she managed, her voice sounding as if she had just come up for air after being under water too long.

He slid his hands up her arms and, curling his lean fingers around her slender shoulders, pulled her towards him gently but inexorably so that the peaks of her breasts touched his chest. She stiffened, every cell in her body screaming out alarm signals as she stared up at him, wide-eyed. In the space of five seconds he had gone from being Graydon Winter, shipping magnate, to Graydon Winter, male animal. . .

'What do you want?' she whispered.

'I've decided what form it's going to take,' he murmured, his thumbs pressing against her neck.

'What form. . .what's going to take?'

'Your punishment—for snooping.'

'Oh, you're being stupid!' Courtenay attempted a laugh, but it didn't quite come off. 'I only looked at a little card, for heaven's sake—it's not as if I'd been poking about in your wallet or——'

'Oh, if you had been poking about in my wallet,' Graydon said mockingly, 'your punishment would have been much more severe. Snooping in a poinsettia plant is only a. . .minor misdemeanour. And the punishment for such a minor misdemeanour is. . .a kiss.'

Though his words were lightly spoken, Courtenay was intensely aware that he wasn't as indifferent as he sounded. His features were taut, his body braced. For a second, she felt bewildered by the contradictory messages he was sending out, then comprehension dawned. Of course! This must be incredibly difficult for him to accept—that he was physically attracted to her when he so despised her. Just as she herself found it incredibly difficult to accept that she was physically attracted to him.

Somehow managing to echo his mocking tone, she

said, 'Surely the accused is allowed an opportunity to say a few words before she's sentenced?'

He ran his palms down her back, his fingertips tracing an erotic, disturbing pattern along her spine before settling on the swell of her buttocks and drawing her against him so that her lower body was trapped inescapably against his. 'I won't deny the prisoner that request.' His voice had an abrasive timbre. 'Go ahead.'

Was she going to be able to go through with this? To get this thing out in the open? She could only try. . . Swallowing, in a vain effort to relieve her tension, she said, 'You seem to be. . .physically attracted to me— and I'm sure you don't want to be. Perhaps it's all right for a man to give in to a sexual attraction where there's no love or even affection involved. . .but in your case it's more complicated. It's not that you have no feelings for me—you hate and despise me. And you're going to end up hating and despising yourself if you're weak enough to give in to your. . .lust. Besides,' she finished with a catch in her voice, 'I find it. . .demeaning. . .to have you paw me like an animal.'

Suddenly she wanted to cry. She could even feel the tears pricking her eyes. Before they could come to fruition, she blinked them away.

He stared down at her, motionless as a statue. And then she saw a strangely tormented expression cross his face. His arms dropped away, and he turned from her. In a grim voice, so low that she could barely hear it, he said, 'Point taken.' Moving back into the office, he swept her jacket off the chair. 'Let's go.'

Courtenay couldn't move for a moment. She just stared at him. She couldn't figure him out at all. Sometimes she hated him. . .but when she had seen that look of anguish in his eyes she had felt all her hatred vanish. . .and she had been almost overcome by a burning desire to take him in her arms and offer him comfort. Comfort? Surely he wasn't in need of comfort? What could there be in Graydon Winter's life—his privileged life—that could possibly cause him unhappiness? He had it all. . .

Didn't he?

'Are you coming?'

His voice scraped against her nerve-endings, jolting her. 'Oh. . .yes.' Courtenay bit her lip, and, avoiding meeting his eyes, walked through to the office.

Not a word passed between them all the way back to Seacliffe, and by the time they reached the house she had a roaring headache. Thankful that there was no one around as they entered the hallway, she slipped off her boots, and, with a quiet, 'Thanks again for taking me to the shipyard,' made for the stairs.

When she reached her room, she closed the door, and, flinging off her jacket, threw it on the bed. Then she walked over to the mirror and stood staring at her reflection, barely recognising herself.

Her eyes had a strange, wild look, her lips were quivering—and her cheeks were every bit as pink as her angora sweater. That *damned* sweater. It had caused her more than enough trouble.

She wrenched the soft garment up over her head and, rolling it into a ball, stuffed it fiercely into the bottom drawer of the dressing-table. Graydon Winter appeared to be fascinated by her breasts, appeared to find them erotically irresistible, and the pink sweater obviously added to the allure.

From now on, she would avoid wearing it. Avoid exciting his desire.

She had meant it when she had said she found his caresses demeaning.

But what she hadn't added was that she found those same caresses exquisitely seductive. She didn't want to provoke him into drawing her into his arms again. If he did, she doubted she'd be able to resist him.

When she went downstairs for breakfast, wearing a baggy blue shirt and taupe slacks, she found he had gone out again.

'Uncle Graydon went to the office,' Vicky said self-importantly. 'He said he had to pick up some notes.'

Alanna darted a frowning glance in Courtenay's direction. 'But he was down there earlier, wasn't he? Livvy told me he'd taken you to the shipyard to see his damaged towboat. Why didn't he pick them up then?'

'He meant to. But they must have—er—slipped his mind, I guess.'

'Well, knowing your Uncle Graydon, child,' Alanna turned to Vicky, 'once he gets to the office, we won't see him for the rest of the day—even though for everyone else this is a holiday!'

Alanna was right. Livvy came through to the drawing-room around eleven, saying Mr Winter had phoned—he was going to be at the office till five, and then he was dining out with Lady Atherton.

They were welcome to each other! Courtenay decided immediately. . .but as she involuntarily pictured Graydon pulling Bertie into an intimate embrace she felt a sharp jab somewhere in the region of her heart. Indigestion, she told herself firmly; jealousy, corrected a sly little voice somewhere deep inside—a voice she scoffed at, then determinedly ignored.

In the afternoon, she took Vicky for a walk while Alanna rested. After dinner, Alanna and Vicky played chess upstairs, and both went to bed around nine.

Courtenay was sitting by the fire in the drawing-room, taking up the hem of Vicky's new dress which she had decided was a couple of inches too long, when she heard the front door crack shut, followed by the sound of Graydon's firm tread in the hall.

She glanced at her watch. It was almost eleven. Surely he would go straight upstairs.

She held her breath, waiting. But a moment later she heard the drawing-room door open. As it shut again, her heart began hammering against her ribcage, and she could feel every nerve-ending in her body scream its awareness of his dark presence as he came up behind her.

CHAPTER EIGHT

'WOULD you like something to drink?'

At Graydon's words, Courtenay looked up and said briefly 'No, thank you.' He was still wearing the casual outfit he'd had on to go to the shipyard that morning, she noticed. His dinner with Bertie obviously hadn't been formal. Had it been at her home—an intimate dinner for two?

As he poured himself a glass of brandy, she turned her gaze again to her sewing, from the corner of her eye seeing the shadow of his lean figure as he moved across the room and lowered himself into the armchair directly opposite her. Peeping from under her lashes, she observed him as he cradled the fine crystal glass in his hands and stared into the leaping flames in the grate.

He paid her no attention till she had sewn the last stitch and had put the needle and thread back into Livvy's sewing-basket. As she folded the dress, smoothing the cream silk collar so that it lay flat, he broke the silence vibrating between them.

'I expect you're going to run away upstairs now.'

'I beg your pardon?'

He shrugged. 'You usually scurry away when I come into a room.'

He was, of course, right. And she had decided only a few seconds ago to go upstairs as soon as she'd finished her sewing. Now, she wouldn't give him that satisfaction. 'Do I?' She looked at him steadily. 'I wasn't planning to scurry anywhere right now.'

He put his drink down on the hearth and, getting to

his feet, began pacing restlessly around the room. Courtenay watched as he stalked to the window, where he pulled the curtains back a few inches and looked out into the dark night. As he turned towards her, a deep frown marred his brow, and he seemed fidgety and on edge.

In an attempt to lighten the atmosphere, Courtenay asked, 'How was your dinner?'

'Dinner at Bertie Atherton's is never less than perfect.' His tone was ironic.

So his lady friend was not only gorgeous, she was also accomplished! Courtenay was ashamed at the twist of envy she felt, and, with an effort, said nonchalantly, 'So she's a wonderful cook?'

Graydon laughed, and it was the first time Courtenay could recall hearing him do so. Startled, she stared at him, noticing with amazement how different he looked when his face wasn't set in grim, scowling lines. Boyish, she thought, and endearing, were the only words to describe him. Lines crinkled around his eyes, and vertical creases slashed his cheeks on either side of his mouth like long dimples.

'No,' he chuckled, 'Bertie Atherton is *not* a wonderful cook. I doubt if the woman knows how to boil water! But she does have pots of money and a direct line to Vancouver's most exclusive caterers!'

She was being utterly bitchy, she knew, but she was delighted to hear she herself could do something that Bertie couldn't! 'So. . .what did you have to eat?'

'Tonight it was Nova Scotia smoked salmon, followed by veal breast with spinach stuffing, and, for dessert, charlotte Malakoff. And Bertie opened a bottle of Dom Perignon because she'd just heard that her brother's coming home from the Amazon some time during the next few days and she wanted to celebrate.'

'Oh, she has a brother? What does he do?'

'John? He's an anthropologist.' A mocking light came into Graydon's eyes. 'You'll enjoy meeting him, since that's the field you want to be in. You should have a lot in common.'

'Not if he's anything like his sister.' The words were out before Courtenay could stop them. 'I'm sorry,' she said flatly, 'that was rude of me. I shouldn't criticise your friends. But Bertie has no interest in talking with someone like me, so I can't imagine that her brother——'

'Someone like you? And what, pray, might *that* be?'

'Different from you, that's for sure!'

'In what way are we different?' he pressed.

'For one thing,' she retorted, 'I don't know what charlotte Malawhatever is——' She broke off with a grimace. 'I'm sorry, that's being flippant, and your question was serious. How are we different? In every important way, I should think, since our family backgrounds couldn't be more different. My father couldn't wait to get me out of his house, and he has absolutely no interest in his grandchild. You, on the other hand, are very proud of your Winter bloodline—your outrageously cavalier method of forcing me to bring Vicky here is proof of that—proof that you'd move heaven and earth to keep her in the bosom of the family—despite the fact that she was conceived out of wedlock.'

'Go on. How else are we different?'

'You use people,' she said bluntly. 'I may not know the names of fancy desserts, and I may never have tasted Dom Perignon—but I'm honest and I have a clear conscience. You treat people like pawns, moving them around to suit yourself, regardless of how it affects them. I don't know how you can sleep nights!' Her voice had been rising as she spoke, now she forced herself to talk more calmly. 'You're just like your brother—that's what he did with me, he used me. He was obsessed with my body, and he used it till he tired of it——'

'Wrong!' Graydon's voice cut into her words with the vicious edge of a butcher's blade. 'He didn't tire of it. He still wanted you, even after——'

As abruptly as he'd started, Graydon stopped, his mouth clamping shut on words he'd obviously never meant to say. Eyes suddenly secretive and shuttered, he turned and, with an angry wrench of his shoulders, moved to the fireplace. His stance was rigid, one arm along the mantel, the other hand rammed into the back pocket of his jeans as he stared blindly into the flames.

For a long moment Courtenay felt stunned, and then as her mind began to function again, she felt a leaden sensation in the pit of her stomach. Dear lord, what had he been going to say? 'He still wanted you, even after. . .'

Even after what? Even after he left you? Were those the words that had stumbled on his lips?

The blood rushed to Courtenay's head, making her dizzy. Graydon had revealed more than he meant to. Had revealed enough to ignite a burning curiosity inside her. What had he meant? Had he and Patrick talked about her, after he'd walked out on their 'marriage'? If so, why hadn't Graydon told her before, when he came to Millar's Lake?

'I don't think we can leave it at that.' Her voice had a fine tremor. 'Finish what you were going to say. Even after. . .*what?*'

He whirled round angrily. 'What a persistent witch you are!' His eyes narrowed grimly as he regarded her. 'But maybe you *should* know.'

'Should know what?' Even as she said the words, Courtenay had a dreadful feeling of premonition that when he answered her question she'd wish she'd never asked it.

'Should know exactly how much damage you did with

your little affair.' He swept back the black hair from his brow. 'I still can't believe Paddy was fool enough to let himself be seduced the way he did, and I promised him I'd never talk about what happened, but he and Beth are both dead now, so what harm is there? You already hate me, I know, but when you hear this, you'll hate me even more. You see——' he gave a dramatic pause for effect '—you see, my lovely, I was the reason Paddy left you.'

Courtenay blinked. What was he talking about? How could he be the reason? He hadn't even known she existed! 'What on earth are you saying?' She shook her head in bewilderment.

Graydon's features were taut, the skin waxy over his nose and cheekbones. 'I'm saying that I knew all about you. I've known all about you for years.'

'But how——'

'I'll tell you how! I found Beth crying one day, and she confided in me that she suspected Paddy was having an affair.' He ignored Courtenay's gasp and went on harshly, 'I was worried about her. . .and, though I didn't believe what she was saying about my brother, to put her mind at rest, I started keeping tabs on him.'

He picked up a paperweight from the sofa table, a glass cube with a seagull imprisoned inside, and hefted it in his hand. 'I noted a definite change in his attitude to Beth, and in the frequency of his trips away from home. After a time, I came to the conclusion that Beth was right. I confronted him privately, and finally he admitted there was another woman.' He swore. 'I almost killed him.'

Courtenay felt a chill creep over her as she listened.

'He finally broke down and admitted everything. Oh, he couldn't tell me much about the woman, because he didn't know too much—she'd kept her background secret. But he told me how they met. He said he'd had too much to drink one night, and this cheap little blonde had picked him up in the bar of the hotel he was staying in, and had tricked him into coming to her room. They spent the night together, and afterwards, when he wanted to get rid of her, he found she was the clinging type and he couldn't——'

'Oh, what a lie!' Courtenay cried. 'It wasn't like that at all! Your brother and I met in one of the parks——'

'I gave him an ultimatum,' Graydon crashed the paperweight down on to the table, the sound reverberating in Courtenay's ears. 'I told him he had to break it off, I didn't care how, and I warned him that if he didn't I'd tell Beth the truth. . .and cut him out of the family business. He agreed.

'I assured Beth she'd been mistaken, and everything went right back to where it had been before.'

'But if everything went back to where it had been before. . .' Courtenay faltered as she remembered what Graydon had said earlier. 'He still wanted you, even after. . .' How could he have, if everything had gone right back to where it had been before?

Graydon's gaze raked cruelly over the blonde hair flowing to her shoulders and the soft swell of her breasts under her blue shirt. 'No, that was a lie—although I didn't know it myself at first—everything didn't quite go back to where it was before. You see, I was wrong about two things. Paddy didn't forget you. I could see it in his eyes sometimes, when I came on him unexpectedly. . .a hunger. . .' Dark colour tinged the pallor of his face. 'And Beth must have seen it too. I thought she'd believed me when I told her Paddy wasn't involved with anyone else. . .but she hadn't. She knew there was another woman, that it was an obsession with him. . .and the knowledge made her ill.'

'Ill? In what way?' Courtenay hardly recognised her own voice.

Graydon moved over to the window. She couldn't see his face, but she could see his hands twisted into fists at his sides as he went on, 'She began drinking. No one else suspected, but I used to find empty gin bottles in a corner of their garage.' He gripped the edge of the windowsill and leaned his forehead against the pane of glass in front of him. 'Poor Beth, she'd never loved anyone but Patrick. She was completely devastated by his infidelity. But I think she might have weathered it, might not have started drinking. . .if she'd known she was pregnant.'

'Pregnant?' Courtenay's lips parted in a shocked exclamation.

'Pregnant,' he gritted out. 'Pregnant with the baby she'd yearned for all her married life. Long before that, she'd finally stopped hoping, and so hadn't been alert to any irregularity, any changes in her body. . .'

Courtenay dug her teeth hard into her lip; she knew what Graydon was going to say, even before he continued, his voice bitter and weary, 'She hadn't known she was carrying Paddy's baby, till she woke up one night and found herself bleeding. By the time Paddy rushed her to hospital, she'd lost the child.'

The hush in the air shrieked in Courtenay's ears as they stared at each other. Her eyes were wide with horror.

And Graydon's. . .

Courtenay could have sworn they glittered with tears as he turned with a hoarse curse and strode from the room. A minute or so later she heard him slam the front door, and shortly after she heard the rev of the car engine.

She sat hunched up in her chair by the fire for a long time after the Mercedes roared away along the drive. She had never met Beth, but she felt her heart ache agonisingly for her. She must have been shattered when she discovered her husband had been unfaithful, but to have suffered the loss of her baby. . .

She, Courtenay, had been betrayed by Patrick too. . .in a different way. . .but she had Vicky.

She knew her own part in the sordid triangle had been completely innocent. . .so why was she feeling the undeniable pricking of guilt deep inside her? Was it because she had let herself fall so blindly in love with Patrick that she hadn't suspected why he wanted such a private wedding? Was it because she had been so naïve that she hadn't even suspected he might have had something to hide when he wouldn't talk about his family?

Thoughts twisted and turned inside her till she thought she would go mad. Finally she put her head down on the arm of the chair, her brow nestled against her forearms, and must have drifted off to sleep, for when she woke later with a start it was to find that the fire had gone out and the room was cold.

Feeling as if she'd aged ten years in an evening, she got slowly to her feet and went upstairs.

She was just coming out of the bathroom in her night-gown ten minutes later when she heard Graydon's tread on the landing, heard a board creak as he stopped outside her door.

Her heart leaped right up into her throat. Stifling a moan of alarm, she skimmed across the carpet in her bare feet, and, flicking off the bedside light, slid hurriedly under the duvet. Seconds later she was lying, eyes tight shut, hair curtaining her face, when the door clicked open.

Her eyelids flickered as the overhead light came on, then she heard the door snap shut. For a moment the tension in the room was so thick that Courtenay thought she might scream. Then it was broken.

'Sit up.' Graydon's voice was low but insistent. 'I want to talk to you.'

Courtenay concentrated on keeping her breathing steady; it was difficult, as her pulse was racing out of control.

She heard him expel a heavy sigh. 'You can cut out the act. The bedroom light was on a moment ago; I saw it as I put the Mercedes into the garage. You couldn't possibly be asleep yet—I came right upstairs.'

Courtenay felt her heart sink. Damn! Why hadn't she thought of that?

She pushed back the covers and sat up, tilting her two pillows against the headboard as she did, and pulling the sheet up to her chin. Then, still blinking a little in the bright light, she looked at him.

He was standing by the dresser in his shirt-sleeves, with his back to her, and she could see his reflection in the mirror as he dragged a weary hand through his black hair. A funny little flutter tightened her throat. He was so heart-stoppingly handsome, and caught off guard like this he appeared young and vulnerable, despite the lines etched on his face. He must have driven somewhere and then gone for a long walk, she thought absently; his skin, previously so drawn and pale, had a healthy glow, and she could have sworn he brought the tang of the sea into the room with him.

She cleared her throat nervously. 'You're right; I wasn't asleep. But I'm glad you want to talk, because I've got something I want to say too.'

He looked up, and their eyes met in the mirror. His were no longer cruel, the way they'd been before, but there was still no spark of friendliness there.

Courtenay curled her fingers over the edge of the sheet as he turned round. 'I can't go on like this,' she said quietly, 'with you treating me the way you have been. In the morning, I shall take Vicky and go back home.'

Graydon pushed himself away from the dresser and approached the bed. He stood looking down at her, his hands hanging by his sides, his eyes grave. 'I want to apologise. I'm sorry.'

It was the last thing she'd expected! But if he was apologising, it must be for a reason. . .some reason that would be to his benefit, certainly not hers! 'Sorry for what?' she asked, her voice cynical.

'I shouldn't have told you about Beth. Though you may have been responsible——'

Courtenay sat up straight as a rod and stared at him through a blur of anger. 'You want to talk—then listen first! It was tragic that your sister-in-law lost the baby she longed for, but I was *not* responsible for——'

'Perhaps not directly——'

'Not even indirectly!' she flared.

'Oh, let's not quibble about it,' he said tiredly. 'We're never going to agree on that point.' He rubbed his right hand in an irritated gesture over his shadowed jaw. 'I don't want you to leave. Alanna seems to have come out of her depression a little since meeting Vicky. But I have to be sure it's not just a temporary improvement, and it's too soon. I'd like you to stay for the two weeks, as we arranged. We'll put the past aside, and try to get along.'

'A little hard, don't you think?' Courtenay's lips curled scornfully.

'Not so hard—you and I need hardly see anything of each other. I leave for the office by seven most mornings, and I'm rarely home before eight or nine in the evening. You and Victoria can spend the mornings with Alanna, and in the afternoons when Alanna's resting a chauffeur will be at your disposal.'

Courtenay's gaze dropped from his. If it weren't for

Alanna, she'd carry out her threat without giving it any more thought. But she knew he was right; his mother did seem happier already, but if they left now she might just sink right back into her earlier depression.

'All right,' she said finally, with slow reluctance, 'I'll agree to stay. . .at least for a day or two to see how things go, but if it doesn't work out then I shall leave.'

She slid down and adjusted the pillows under her head. Pulling the duvet to her chin, she closed her eyes. As far as she was concerned, the conversation was over.

Graydon must have thought so too, for he didn't answer. But for the longest time she didn't hear a sound, and she was just about to sit up and demand to know why he wasn't leaving, when she heard his tread on the carpet, and a moment later the door clicked shut behind him.

Graydon stayed away from early morning till late evening for the next couple of days. Courtenay in turn made a point of getting Vicky to bed by eight, and going to her own room before Graydon came home. She knew it was for the best, knew that in the light of the powerful physical attraction that crackled so dangerously between them nothing was to be gained by being in each other's company.

She tried not to think of how the hours dragged, tried not to notice how she was always straining for the sound of his step in the hall. . .

And then on the third morning she found herself knocking urgently on his bedroom door around six o'clock. She knew he was awake—she had heard him running the shower just a few minutes before—and, trying to quell her feelings of panic, she waited for him to answer.

When he opened his door, he had nothing on but a white bathtowel wrapped around his waist. His damp hair clung to his forehead, and water glistened on his tanned shoulders, and in the crisp curls matting his chest.

'You! What the devil's up?' He frowned, his gaze flickering over the pink robe she had thrown on in such haste.

'It's Vicky,' Courtenay said breathlessly. 'She isn't at all well. Her throat's sore and she has a dreadful headache. Maybe I'm over-reacting, but ever since her pneumonia I go slightly hysterical whenever——'

'Does she have a fever?'

'She's burning up, and she tells me all her bones are aching.' Courtenay swept a hand distraughtly through her tousled hair. 'I hate to impose on you, but I wondered if you could take us to the emergency department at the hospital, or perhaps I could call a cab——'

'Is she having difficulty breathing?'

'No. . .no, she's not. It's just that——'

'Come in here a minute.' Graydon held open the door of his bedroom, and, as she hesitated, he motioned impatiently for her to go in. 'I know you're worried and I understand your concern, but let's not over-react. I'm going to call Frank Scott, our family doctor. He lives two minutes from here.'

Courtenay clasped her arms around her waist to stop herself from shivering as Graydon strode across to the phone on his nightstand. Holding the receiver to his ear, he punched a number, and seconds later he said,

'Frank, Graydon Winter here. Apologies for calling you so early. Look, my nine-year-old niece is with us for the holidays——' He broke off, listening for a moment before saying tautly, 'She's Patrick's child—I'll explain later. She's come down with something—sore throat, headache, fever. Could you have a look at her?' He paused a moment, then said, 'Great, see you in five minutes.'

As he replaced the receiver, Courtenay said, 'Thank you so much. I can't tell you how I appreciate your help.'

'No problem.' He gestured towards the door. 'Off you go now, and let me get dressed before Frank gets here.'

'I didn't know there were still doctors who made house calls——'

Graydon looked at her with a sardonic twist of his dark eyebrows. 'Money does have its uses, doesn't it?'

So even at a time like this he couldn't refrain from baiting her. But Courtenay didn't feel any anger as she hurried back to Vicky's room; what Graydon thought of her didn't matter. . .at least, not at this moment. All that mattered was Vicky. She felt her heart beat faster as she opened the bedroom door and saw her daughter lying against the pillows, her cheeks bright scarlet.

'Your uncle Graydon's doctor will be here soon.' Courtenay managed a reassuring smile.

'Goody,' Vicky croaked. 'I hope he can make me feel better.'

Dr Scott was a young man with a Liverpudlian accent, a cheery manner, and twinkling grey eyes. Graydon ushered him into Vicky's bedroom and introduced him to Courtenay and Vicky before going downstairs again.

The doctor spent some time checking Vicky thoroughly before he finally put his stethoscope away. 'I'm afraid you're going to have to stay in bed for a few days, young lady,' he said with mock severity as Vicky tugged down her pyjama top. He scribbled a prescription on his pad, and, tearing it off, handed it to Courtenay. 'I'll pop back to see her tomorrow.' He looked down at Vicky. 'And don't worry, your medicine is cherry-flavoured; you'll love it!'

As Courtenay escorted him down to the hall, Graydon appeared from the direction of the drawing-room.

'She's caught a particularly vicious bug that's going the rounds.' Dr Scott addressed them both. 'And with the child's history of pneumonia we'll keep a good eye on her. She'll probably have to stay indoors for the best part of a week—no point in letting her go out too soon and risking a relapse.'

After he left, Graydon closed the front door and walked back across the hall towards Courtenay, who had lingered at the foot of the stairs, waiting for him.

'I'm afraid,' she said quietly, 'I'm going to have to ask you for another favour.'

'You have a prescription you want filled?'

She nodded. 'I hate to impose on you like this, but——'

'For heaven's sake!' he exploded, his black brows lowered fiercely. 'Victoria's my niece—I'm only too glad to do anything I can for her. Do you think I'm some kind of monster? Here. . .' He flung out one hand in a furious and impatient gesture. 'Give me the damned thing!'

Normally, when confronted by Graydon's hostility, Courtenay was more than able to defend herself. But her anxiety over Vicky had left her feeling weak and shaky, and, to her dismay, Graydon's fierce explosion brought tears to her eyes. Lowering her lashes to hide her distress, she held out the prescription.

The scrap of paper rustled as he took it and stuffed it into one of his trouser pockets. 'I'll phone around to see which pharmacy is open,' he said tersely. 'I should be back within half an hour or so.'

'Thanks,' Courtenay whispered, and turned away.

Hard fingers grasped her shoulders and wrenched her round to face him again. Capturing her chin between the thumb and forefinger of his right hand, Graydon forced her head up, and as he saw the shine of her unshed tears he uttered an exasperated exclamation.

'Maybe I *am* some kind of a monster,' he growled, 'shouting at you when you're upset!'

His eyes swirled with the rich blue-green of petrol spilled on a wet road. In some distant part of Courtenay's mind, she knew she should be tearing herself from his grasp, but she couldn't. All she could do was stare up helplessly into those hypnotic, beautiful eyes.

'Dear lord, you're doing it again,' he said, his voice a mingling of desire and despair.

'Doing what?' Courtenay's legs felt suddenly weak.

'Looking at me as if you're waiting to be kissed!' He released her chin, but before she had realised she was free to move back he had framed her face in his strong hands. 'Are you?' He stepped closer so that their bodies almost touched. 'Waiting to be kissed?'

'No,' she whispered. *Liar*, a little voice inside her protested.

'Liar,' Graydon's murmured voice echoed, seconds before his mouth sought and claimed hers.

He smelled of shaving cream and soap, and his skin was as smooth as the finest leather. His lips were warm and full—their taste now exquisitely familiar. Courtenay knew she could have pulled away, knew she *should* have pulled away, but instead she found her own lips softening and clinging as his mouth moved with sensual urgency over hers. The hands which had been framing her face now wove through her hair, capturing her, tilting her head so that he had complete control over the angle of their kiss. Courtenay swayed towards him, closing her eyes, and it seemed natural to put her arms around him, to savour the soft texture of his shirt with her fingertips.

He lifted his lips for a moment, and her lashes fluttered open. He was staring down at her, his eyes dark with yearning. 'You're irresistible,' he murmured. 'You are just so damned irresistible.'

A flame of fire licked along Courtenay's veins. He found her irresistible. . .just as she found him. He pulled her closer, and she could feel every hard line of his body against her own, through the soft fabric of her robe and the flimsy nylon of her nightie. Every cell in her body sang in sweet surrender——

'Mom! I'd like a cold drink.'

Courtenay jerked herself away from Graydon as she heard Vicky's croaking voice. Looking up, she saw her daughter at the head of the stairs, her cheeks as bright red as her polo pyjamas. 'All right, honey.' She managed a smile, but her words trembled. 'I'm coming.'

Graydon's voice was imbued with frustration as it followed her up the stairs. 'I'll see you when I get back with the medicine.'

How long had Vicky been standing there before she called downstairs? Courtenay wondered distraughtly a few moments later as she held a glass of iced water to her daughter's lips. Had she seen the kiss? With a heavy sigh, she put the empty glass on the nightstand and tucked Vicky's limp body under the covers again. What would have happened between Graydon and herself had Vicky not chosen that moment to interrupt?

She had told Graydon, when he had asked her on Boxing Night to stay for the two weeks originally planned for, that she'd give it a couple of days and if things didn't work out, she'd leave. Things were *not* working out, but. . .

Courtenay closed her eyes. No matter how desperately she wanted to leave, to extricate herself from the web of desire in which she and Graydon were trapped, she couldn't. Not any longer. Not with Vicky so sick.

Dr Scott had recommended that his patient stay indoors for a week. In view of Vicky's previous bout of pneumonia, Courtenay knew she couldn't take any risks where her daughter's health was concerned. She wouldn't dream of travelling with her till she was quite better. That meant she was stuck at Seacliffe for at least another seven days.

They would, she knew, be the longest seven days of her life.

CHAPTER NINE

COURTENAY was in Vicky's bedroom around two-thirty that afternoon when Graydon came home from the office early. She didn't hear him come into the house—didn't even hear him come up the stairs. She was sitting on the edge of Vicky's bed, singing softly and watching her daughter's eyelids slowly close, when she felt an uneasy prickle at her nape.

The lullaby died in her throat. Twitching her head round, she felt a tremor break the even rhythm of her heartbeats as she saw Graydon standing in the doorway, dressed in a navy pinstriped suit with a white shirt and a navy and mauve silk tie. His hair was slightly wind-tousled, giving him a rakish look that plucked at her senses, and for a brief, flashing moment she surprised in his eyes the same look of desire that had been there that morning. . .a look of such naked, raw wanting that she felt her stomach muscles clench in convulsive response.

Somehow she managed to keep her features composed. Getting up from the bed, she tucked the tail of her emerald green shirt into her jeans with a deliberately casual gesture before walking across the room. Graydon held the door open for her, and as she threw him another quick glance she saw—as she had expected—that his eyes were once again cool and shuttered.

'How is she?' he murmured.

'She's had a very restless day—I hope she'll feel better after she has a sleep.' She felt Graydon's narrowed gaze on her face as he pulled the door quietly shut.

'You could do with a rest yourself,' he said brusquely. 'You look absolutely washed out.'

Just what she needed to hear, Courtenay thought tiredly. With the back of one hand she brushed aside a wisp of damp hair that had fallen over one eye. 'I'll be all right once I've had a cup of coffee to perk me up.'

'Where's Alanna?'

'She's napping. . .and Livvy's gone out with Wheeler to get groceries.'

Graydon grasped her by the elbow. 'I want you to go down to the drawing-room and put your feet up.' He led her towards the stairs, and as they descended he said tersely, 'I'll get your coffee.'

Courtenay's automatic reaction was to refuse, but his offer was just too tempting; anxiety about Vicky had knocked the stuffing right out of her, and in addition her daughter had been a very fractious, demanding patient and had run her ragged all morning. 'Thanks, I'd appreciate that.'

At the foot of the stairs, Graydon dropped her arm and said, 'I'll only be a few minutes.'

The drawing-room was empty and a cheerful fire crackled in the grate. Moving over to the hearth, Courtenay kicked off her slippers, and, dropping into one of the armchairs, tucked her feet under her. Closing her eyes, she found her thoughts inexorably returning to the moment in the bedroom when Graydon had stared at her with such hungry yearning. She let her head fall against the padded wing of the chair and wondered miserably why she felt like crying. She had shed so many tears after Patrick had betrayed her that she had believed none were left to shed—now his brother was proving her wrong. When Graydon was around, she seemed to disintegrate into a weepy——

The sound of the door opening cracked into her

unhappy reflections, and, looking round, to her surprise she saw Bertie Atherton coming through the doorway.

The redhead stopped short when she saw Courtenay. 'Oh,' she said sourly, '*you're* here. I expected to find——'

'Graydon's in the kitchen.' Courtenay skimmed a glance over the other woman's outfit, a butter-soft gold leather bomber jacket, and matching trousers which looked as if they'd been spray-painted on to her slender legs. 'He's making me a cup of coffee.'

For just a second, Bertie looked startled. Then, toying with one of her gold hoop earrings, she walked forward with a smile—if such an artificial drawing back of the lips could be called a smile, Courtenay thought derisively.

The redhead stood over her, slim hips tilted at an elegant angle. 'I came to borrow some of his tapes for my New Year's Eve party tomorrow night,' she drawled. 'But I'm glad to have the opportunity to talk with you alone. Graydon tells me he's invited you to come to the party——'

'That's right, but——'

'As I'm sure you've guessed, he's just being polite. He probably feels it would be rude to go out and leave you here alone. Of course, he's quite wrong, since this party was planned long before your arrival at Seacliffe. Besides, I *know* you'd rather not come—it's obvious we move in different worlds, and you just wouldn't fit in. Not to mention that you won't know a soul and it'll be rather boring.'

So Graydon hadn't told Bertie she had turned down his invitation to the New Year's party! Well, thought Courtenay mischievously, she'd keep the other woman stewing for a bit.

'Really?' She cocked an astonished eyebrow in Bertie's direction. 'How strange! Why on earth would you go to all the bother and expense of organising a party only to advertise it as being *boring*?'

Bertie's face flushed angrily. 'That's not what I meant,' she snapped. 'It certainly won't be boring for my friends. You see, our crowd will all be there—the old ski crowd, that is. It's our first social get-together since my return from England in the spring after Alex's death, and we're looking forward immensely to reminiscing over old times.' Her narrow shoulders lifted in a superior, affected shrug. 'We all skied at Whistler together for years—Patrick organised the first weekend, and it was such a success that. . .'

The rest of Bertie's words didn't register on Courtenay's brain; her attention was focused solely on what the other woman had just said. . .about 'the ski crowd'. She felt a seed of excitement sprout to life inside her. It was while Patrick was at Whistler on one of those weekends that she had met him. Would his friend—the one who had pretended to be a marriage commissioner—be at the party?

An image flickered in her brain. . .a very vague image of the man who had read the words of the marriage ceremony. So vague it was hard to recall even his colouring. She had been so intoxicated with happiness that day that she'd barely had eyes for anyone except Patrick. But surely if she saw the man again she would recognise him. . .

A shivering breath escaped her as she made a reckless decision. She would go to the party. Wouldn't it be a triumph if she was able to point to the impostor and say to Graydon, *There's* the man who 'married' Patrick and me?

She blinked as she realised Bertie was still talking.

'So,' the other woman finished with a supercilious curl of her upper lip, 'all you have to do is tell Graydon that you'd rather stay home than be bored.'

Courtenay dipped her lashes to hide the shine of excitement in her eyes. 'No, Bertie,' she twined her fingers together in her lap, 'I shan't be bored.' And then, driven by some spontaneous spark of devilment, she added in a husky, suggestive voice, 'I'll be with Graydon—how could I possibly be bored in the company of such a devastatingly attractive and sexy man?'

In the stunned silence that followed, Courtenay could hear the windowpane tremble in the breeze from the ocean. When finally she looked up, she found herself stifling a gasp as she saw that Graydon was standing just inside the doorway.

How long had he been there? Courtenay felt her heart drum against her ribs. Had he heard what she had just said? Of course he had—there was a look of mocking challenge in his blue-green eyes that left her in no doubt. For an endless moment she felt as if they were the only people in the room; electric currents vibrated between them with such force that it took her breath away.

Then Graydon moved, and the spell was broken. As she sat numbly, he strode forward with a casual 'Hi, there, Bertie—you let yourself in, I see.'

Bertie spun round on her heel, the alarm in her eyes testifying to her anxiety as to whether or not Graydon had overheard what *she* had said. His bland look gave no sign of it, and Courtenay thought she heard a little sigh of relief.

She didn't look up at Graydon as she took the mug of coffee from him, only murmuring, 'Thank you,' but she felt a zing of sensation tingle up her arm as his thumb brushed the back of her hand. Had the touch happened accidentally? She thought not; it had been too firm, too lingering.

'Yes, darling—I came by to borrow the tapes you promised me for my party.' The redhead's amber gaze clung to Graydon. 'I know you said you'd bring them tomorrow night, but I happened to be in the area and——'

'Sorry, Bertie, I haven't looked them out yet—but don't worry, I won't forget to take them along.' Graydon shrugged off his jacket and threw it on to one of the chairs. 'Now, I've made a pot of coffee—would you like some?'

Bertie shook her head. 'No, I can't wait. John's going to arrive any day now, and I want to be home when he does.'

'I'll see you to your car, then.'

As Graydon and Bertie walked from the room, Courtenay watched them bleakly. They made such a striking couple—both so attractive, both wearing their expensive clothes so elegantly. With a sigh, she acknowledged that Bertie had been right—she, Courtenay, would never fit into the world to which they belonged. Not that she even wanted to, but she couldn't help wondering—wistfully, and just for a moment—what it would be like to be 'one of the old ski crowd', to be accepted by Graydon as a friend. . .

With an abrupt exclamation, she halted her train of thought. She didn't want to be one of Graydon Winter's friends. All she wanted to do was set the record straight before she left for Millar's Lake in a few days. And if things went as she hoped at the party, then she and Vicky——

Vicky! Cupping her mug in her hands, she stared frustratedly into space, all her earlier excitement at the thought of finding the 'marriage commissioner' dissipating like mist under a blazing sun. What a fool she was— what a dreamer! How could she possibly go to a party tomorrow night? She couldn't leave Vicky, not when her daughter was so ill.

Her mouth drooped as disappointment coursed

through her. The one chance to prove that she'd been telling the truth, and she couldn't take it.

But why did she care? Why was it so important to her that Graydon believe her story? She wanted nothing more than to go back to Millar's Lake and forget about him. . .

Didn't she?

An answer to her question echoed in her brain, but she didn't listen to it. It was an answer she didn't want to hear.

Next morning, Vicky seemed a little better. She spent most of the afternoon dozing and around five o'clock, when Courtenay took her temperature, it was almost normal. Courtenay had just finished putting her into a clean nightie when there was a brief knock at the bedroom door. It opened, and Graydon came in.

With him he had brought a box from one of Vancouver's department stores. . .and when he extricated a portable TV set and laid it on Vicky's dressing-table the child stared at it disbelievingly.

'Oh, thank you, Uncle Graydon!' Her voice, still weak and slightly hoarse, trembled with excitement. 'A TV of my very own—just wait till I show my friend Amy!'

'We won't be taking it back to Millar's Lake, honey.' Courtenay felt a flush of embarrassment colour her cheeks. 'Your uncle is just letting you use it while you're here.'

'No, it's Victoria's.' Graydon plugged the set into a wall outlet and switched it on. 'A late Christmas present.'

'See, Mom,' Vicky pushed herself up on her elbows, her face beaming as she saw the picture begin to appear on the screen, 'it *is* mine! Yippee!'

'I'm sorry, Vicky, I can't allow you to accept it——'

'Whyever not?' Resentful tears welled up in Vicky's blue eyes. 'Is it because we haven't known Uncle Graydon for very long?'

'Well,' Courtenay hesitated, 'yes, I guess that's the main r——'

'But you were kissing!' Brushing aside her tears, Vicky stared indignantly at her mother. 'I *saw* you— yesterday morning, at the foot of the stairs. I know you've told me never to take presents from strangers, but how can Uncle Graydon be a stranger if you let him kiss you?'

Courtenay could feel Graydon's gaze challenging her. Taking a deep breath, she faced him. 'Could I talk with you for a moment?' she asked grimly. '*Alone?*'

'Sure.' Unearthing a remote control clicker from the box, he tossed it casually to Vicky. 'Here, I'll send Livvy up with the *TV Guide*. Your mother and I are going out to a party tonight—perhaps you can find a good movie to watch.'

Anger swelled up inside Courtenay as she stalked from the room. What she had to say to Graydon she didn't want Vicky to hear. She stormed downstairs, and into the drawing-room, where, hands clenched into fists, she took up a stance at the hearth with her back to the fire.

A moment later Graydon came in, closing the door behind him.

'Two things,' Courtenay snapped, before he was halfway across the room. 'Firstly, I will not allow Vicky to accept any more expensive presents, and secondly——'

'Let's deal with your problems one at a time.' Graydon threw himself down on the sofa, and sprawled lazily with his arms stretched out along the back, and his right leg crossed over the left at the knee. 'The TV set. As you must know, I can well afford it——'

'That,' Courtenay interrupted scathingly, 'is not the point. Vicky is a very contented child. . .or has been, up till now. When I take her home to Millar's Lake, I don't want that to change—I don't want her to start wanting things I can't afford. I may be a single mother, but I will never accept charity!'

'Charity?' Graydon flung himself to his feet and glared at her. 'For heaven's sake, Courtenay, this is my niece we're talking about!' He paced across to the window, where he stood staring out for several moments before he turned back again, his features set in taut lines. 'Have you ever wondered about Patrick's estate?'

His question, coming out of the blue as it did, threw Courtenay momentarily. 'Patrick's estate? You mean. . .' She frowned. 'You mean. . .who he left his money to?'

Graydon's lips tightened. 'Exactly.'

Courtenay shrugged. 'No, I haven't. What does that have to do with me?'

'Not you—Victoria. As his daughter, his only child, she would stand to inherit whatever he left.'

'I don't *want*——'

'At any rate, he left nothing, so the question of what *you* want doesn't arise. But had he not lost every red cent in the last recession, Victoria would have been heir to a substantial sum. How would you have felt about that?'

Courtenay felt a rush of relief as Graydon finished talking. No, she hadn't ever thought about Patrick's estate, but she was thankful things had turned out the way they had. It would have been devastating to her pride in her hard-won independence to know that one day Vicky would inherit money from a man she herself despised.

'Do you really want to know?' She levelled a steady glance at him. 'I would have felt sick to my stomach.

But I must contradict you on one point. You're wrong when you state that Patrick left nothing. He left *me* something. . .or rather, somebody. He left me Vicky. My Winter legacy.' Courtenay's lips curved ironically. '*My* Winter legacy, Graydon. And I shall be the one who makes decisions regarding her welfare. In this instance—the TV set—she may of course use it while we're here, and I do appreciate your thoughtfulness— but it will stay at Seacliffe when we go home.'

Ignoring his frustrated exclamation, and before he could argue, she went on coolly, 'The second thing I want to talk about is Bertie's party tonight. I'm not going.'

He cocked a taunting eyebrow at her. 'Why have you changed your mind? Didn't I hear you tell Bertie that you expected to have a good time because you'd be with—let me see if I can remember how you put it. . .ah, yes. . ."such a devastatingly attractive and sexy man"?'

Courtenay felt her cheeks grow warm. 'I'm sure you know quite well I said that only to annoy Bertie. She was——'

'Asking for it?'

'As a matter of fact, yes, she was asking for it.' Courtenay nodded grimly. 'But I can't go to the party— I'd be nervous about leaving Vicky when she isn't well.'

'I've already anticipated—and overcome—that hurdle. Livvy's sister Jan is a nurse—she's coming round to spend the night here, and she and Livvy will be delighted to babysit.'

'But——'

'Even a mother's not indispensable, Courtenay. Victoria will survive.'

Courtenay hesitated. She longed to tell him she wouldn't accompany him, but suddenly—once again— the vague image of Patrick's friend flickered through her mind. Would he be at the party? It was a small chance, but it might perhaps be the only one she'd ever have to prove to Graydon that she hadn't lied about the fake marriage. Before she could respond to what he had said, he went on,

'And don't come up with the tired old excuse that you have nothing to wear. You have the black dress. Oh, I know how you feel about my buying it for you,' he added swiftly before she could protest, 'so I'm not telling you to wear it. I'm *asking* you to, as a special favour to me.'

A special favour. Well, that must be a first—Graydon Winter requesting a favour! And it was a favour she found hard to refuse, since she really did have nothing at all suitable to wear! 'All right,' she said quietly, 'I'll go to the party. . .and I'll wear the black dress.'

'Good.' There was no mistaking the smugness in his tone.

'But *I'll* pay for it—even if it takes me ten years, and even if I never wear it again!'

He opened his mouth to argue, but Courtenay saw him close it again when he noticed the adamant squaring of her shoulders. He shrugged, and she knew the matter was settled. But she still had a question. . .

'What I don't understand is why you want to take me to the party in the first place.'

His eyes became veiled. 'I have my reasons.'

'And those reasons are?'

The stubborn set of his jaw was her only answer.

'All right,' she said, 'but I too have my reasons.' She finished her coffee and stood up. 'And before the night's out I hope to be able to share them with you.'

There was no mistaking the flicker of curiosity in his eyes as she sailed past him on her way to the door.

Courtenay hissed out an exasperated sigh. Leaning towards her reflection in the mirrored door of the

bedroom closet, she tugged impatiently at her white
bra, but regardless of her attempts to hide the straps,
they still peeped impudently from the low-cut neckline
of the velvet dress.

There was no way it would do. If only she'd had a
black one, it wouldn't have been so noticeable—she
might have got away with it. She muttered a mild curse
under her breath—there was nothing for it but to go to
the party bra-less.

Sliding down the back zip of her dress, she wriggled
out of the slinky garment and tossed it on the chair
beside her. Her breasts jutted out freely as she unhooked
the offending bra and tossed it on to the dressing-table,
where the hooks skittered on the surface with a metallic
clatter. The sound must have concealed the click of the
bedroom door opening, for her first intimation that
someone had come into the room was Graydon's
impatient voice.

'For heaven's sake, Courtenay, what's keeping——?'

The words halted abruptly. And in the space of a
second, in the mirror, Courtenay was confronted with
two wildly contrasting images. . .

First, her own reflection. Hair flowing past her
shoulders in a smooth blonde swathe, pink-painted lips
parted in dismay, mascaraed eyes round with disbelief. . . With her naked pink-tipped breasts, sheer black
tights shadowing her legs and thighs, and her high-
heeled black sandals, she knew she couldn't have presented a more erotic picture.

Graydon obviously agreed. Snapping the door shut
behind him, he leaned against it, his dark eyes wide and
unblinking as if someone had just stunned him with a
near-lethal blow to the head. He couldn't have been
more devastated, Courtenay thought dizzily as she
stared at his reflection—nor more devastating! He was

wearing a beautifully cut black tuxedo with silk-trimmed lapels, a white-on-white shirt with silver glinting at the cuffs, and a red bow-tie with matching cummerbund.

Courtenay took it all in, in the one brief, slippery second before she whirled round to face him, blood draining from her face, her arms flying up to cross over her naked breasts.

'I. . . I'm sorry if I kept you waiting.' She didn't recognise her own voice! That strangled whisper. . .

'No need to apologise.' Each word was an invitation, a sensual caress. Pushing himself away from the door, he began walking slowly towards her, his gaze never leaving her even when he bent to scoop her dress from the chair. 'It seems my timing couldn't have been better—you obviously need some help getting ready.'

He came so close that Courtenay could smell the scent of his aftershave. . .an intoxicating scent that made her knees feel weak.

'Give me the dress.' She held out one trembling arm, keeping the other over her breasts. 'I don't need any help.'

The black velvet blurred before her eyes as he swished the garment behind him. 'What's the magic word?' he taunted softly.

'*Please.*' She swayed away from him as he reached out one hand to touch her hair, and his fingertips grazed her cheek, making her shiver. 'You had no right to walk in here——'

'I didn't know you were still dressing. You were ready when Livvy came downstairs ten minutes ago. She told me. . .'

'I *was* ready to come down then,' she said unsteadily, 'or rather I thought I was, but I hadn't realised my bra was going to show, so I had to take it off. I don't have a black one here with me. . . I'll have to go without a bra. . .or maybe I should stay home after all. . .'

Why was she babbling so? Was she afraid that if she stopped talking the silence in the room would leave space for the sexual tension that was sizzling between them, ready to explode? 'Just go,' she pleaded. 'I'll be downstairs in a minute.'

'Mm-mm.' Graydon's eyes glittered as he shook his head. 'I'm not going anywhere. At least, not until you're ready to come with me—I promised Bertie I'd get there early with the tapes, and we're already late. I shall stay and make sure you don't waste any more time. . . In fact, I think I'd better dress you myself. That way——' he ignored her protesting exclamation '—that way, I'll be sure you won't spend any more time dallying.'

Courtenay knew he meant it; she also knew she wasn't strong enough to fight him off physically. And she didn't think she could stand being in the same room with him for much longer, in this half-nude state, without her body revealing how his closeness was affecting her.

'All right,' she said stiffly. 'Get on with it.'

His lips twisted in a sardonic smile. 'You'll have to co-operate. Put out your arms.'

For a long moment Courtenay glared at him; or rather, she tried to glare at him. She found it impossible to hold on to her anger and frustration as she felt herself begin to drown in the beautiful blue-green eyes. . .eyes that were rapidly becoming smoky with desire. Squeezing her eyelids tightly shut, she forced her thoughts to focus on something else. . .anything else. . .while she fumbled for the sleeves of the dress. But even with her eyes closed she could have sworn she felt his gaze caress her nakedness. Was that a harshly indrawn breath. . .?

She clamped her jaws together and tried to concentrate on the feel of the velvet as it was slipped over her arms, over her head, and glided caressingly down her

body. As soon as she was covered, she opened her eyes
and dragged her hair from her face.

'I can zip it myself!' She tried to push Graydon's
hands away as he placed them firmly on her shoulders.

'I'll do it.' He turned her round so that she had her
back to him. There was no mistaking the authority—
certainly no mistaking the sexy huskiness—in his tone.

Courtenay was hypnotised by their reflection in the
mirror; his head was bent, his brow furrowed as he
carefully drew up the zip. She felt his fingers brush her
spine as he fastened the little hook at the top, and a
tingle danced across her skin. With her breath held
tautly in her lungs, she waited for him to step away.

He didn't.

He turned her towards him again, and before she
could resist he'd pulled her against him so firmly that
she could feel his jacket buttons against her ribcage. She
heard him groan as he threaded his hands through her
hair, but as he lowered his lips towards hers she jerked
her head to the side.

'You know how late we are already.' Her voice had a
distinct tremor. 'And I want to check on Vicky
before——'

'Victoria is fine.' His words were almost lost as he
buried his face in her scented hair. 'She's watching TV.
You'll get to see her in a minute, but first we——'

'First we nothing!' Courtenay tried to free herself, but
he tightened his grip, and began kissing the sensitive
area below her ear. 'Your perfume. . .' His tone held a
faint hint of surprise. 'I'd somehow expected you to
wear something more. . .sultry. I don't recognise this
fragrance.'

'It's new,' Courtenay said tersely. 'It's called Get
Lost. You've probably never encountered it before.'

She heard him chuckle, and, despite herself, felt her
own lips twitching. Irritated, she made another attempt

to jerk herself away from him, but his hands slid along her neck, his thumbs capturing her under each ear, so that it hurt to move. She could feel the familiar stirrings inside her, stirrings stimulated by the touch of his fingertips on her skin. . .

Stirrings that triggered a small moan in her throat. His body stilled for a moment, and then, cupping her face with his hands, he ran a cloudy gaze over her features. He frowned. 'You're far too pale.' His tone was dangerously soft. 'We can't have you going to a party looking like a ghost. What you need is a thorough kissing to——'

'Don't bother!' Courtenay countered heatedly. 'I'd rather look like a ghost than have you maul me.'

'Maul you? Oh, I don't intend to maul you. What I do intend to do is this. . .'

His lips claimed hers with a mastery that blotted out all her thoughts and drained all the strength from her legs. She teetered on her high heels, clutching towards him automatically for support. His jacket had fallen further open as he embraced her, and as her palms slid over his ribcage, her hands met firm, tautly muscled flesh, over which was stretched the very finest silk.

She felt as if her fingertips were scorched, but before she could pull them away Graydon lifted her closer, trapping her arms between them. He clamped her to him so tightly that her breath seemed to be squeezed right out of her body.

She tore her lips away from his. 'Don't!' she gasped, raising her eyes pleadingly. 'Please, don't. . .'

Her tremulous appeal faded to nothing as their gazes locked, locked with an impact that set her head reeling. Oh, those eyes—they seemed to pull her into his very soul. For the first time, she noticed yellow flecks twinkling like gold dust in the blue-green.

And then his mouth swooped down to capture hers

again. Dear heavens, she'd never experienced anything like this! Electricity surged through her body, its intensity almost painful. Everywhere he was touching her, she felt the fire blaze between them. His warm palms cradled her fevered cheeks, his thighs burned against her velvet-clad body. . .

His lips, so often thin with disapproval, seemed to gain a rich fullness as they worked their sensual magic, and it was a magic which made her respond in an abandoned way that horrified her. Her body defiantly disobeyed the orders she was frantically sending it; it wanted to become part of his. . .it clung to him, moulded itself against his hard contours, shamelessly. . .

She knew, in some distant part of her mind, that she would never, as long as she lived, forget this moment. . .or forget the taste of him—the sweetness and the wildness—and the unique male essence of him that filled her with an aching need to be possessed, a need heightened to exquisite agony as he began a slow erotic movement with his hips, a movement which was orchestrated in time with the relentless demands of his tongue which he had coaxed between her parted lips. . .

Courtenay felt the soft duvet under her as he gently lowered her to sit on the bed, felt the mattress give as he sank down beside her. How had they got there? She hadn't been aware that they had moved across the room.

She was powerless to resist as he slid the zip of her dress down again, powerless to resist as he brushed the sensuous velvet folds of the dress to her waist, powerless to resist as he lowered her to lie back on the pillows. Absently, as if the sound came from another world, she was aware of the ring of a phone somewhere in the distance.

Graydon leaned over her, supported on either side by his hands on the mattress, and began to kiss her again.

Not till her mouth was swollen and bruised did his lips finally slide from hers, to trail lingeringly over her throat, over her collarbone, to the swell of her breasts.

Courtenay felt blood pulsating to the sensitive peaks, and waited agonisingly for the warm seeking lips to find their goal. First they captured one tight bud and then the other, worshipping each in turn. She moaned, twisting her head from side to side, while he sipped as if they were tiny perfect roses fashioned just for him. And as if he alone, with his uniquely tender touch, could make them flower.

'Dear lord,' she managed an agonised murmur, 'don't do that. . . Stop! We should be going. . .'

His fingers were threaded through the hair coiling damply over her bare shoulder. 'I know.' Thick, husky, his answer held no conviction whatsoever.

'My dress. . . It's going to be crushed. . .'

'Don't worry. . .'

'Let me get up.'

'Soon. . .'

'Now. . .'

'After——'

After? After what?

After he had made love to her? After he had used her?

Courtenay reeled from the implications of the questions that had thrust themselves into her mind. Hadn't she sworn never to let herself be lured into this type of situation again? Hadn't she learned *anything* from her experience with Patrick? If she hadn't, then she deserved whatever happened to her. She deserved the pain and the humiliation that would surely follow if she were to give in to the crazy, reckless urgings of her body.

Adrenalin surged through her veins, giving her the extra strength she needed to wrench herself from under him. Heedless of his startled exclamation, she rolled off the bed and stumbled away, to stand in the middle of the room. Pulling up her dress with shaky fingers, she stared at him apprehensively, her heart beating as if it was going to burst as he flung himself up and followed her. He was just a few feet away when someone knocked on the bedroom door.

For a shocked moment, they both froze. Then Graydon said 'Yes?' His voice was harsh.

'Lady Atherton's on the phone.' Livvy's words drifted to their ears. 'She's waiting for the tapes you promised.'

Graydon clenched his fists at his side. 'Tell her we're on our way.'

Courtenay could hear Livvy run down the stairs, the light steps on the uncarpeted steps punctuated by Graydon's strained breathing. She heard him curse softly.

Her fingers trembled as she pulled up the zip of her dress. 'Shall we go, then?' she asked, trying to mask her embarrassment with a bright, airy tone.

'Courtenay. . .' Graydon took a step towards her, his eyes still cloudy with passion. 'Wait!'

'Why?' Courtenay swung away from him and walked to the mirror, where she finger-combed her hair deftly. 'Look at me,' she said in a gay tone, 'you said I was pale. . . I'm glowing now, aren't I?'

She pirouetted to face him, hoping the shine in her eyes would be interpreted as innocent excitement. 'You did a good job, Graydon.' She swallowed a sudden lump in her throat as she saw the white tension lines appear around his nostrils. Running a smoothing hand down over her hips, she forced herself to walk away from him, across the room. 'You succeeded splendidly. No one is going to mistake me for a ghost tonight! Now. . .' She opened the door and moved down the hallway, calling back over her shoulder, 'I'll go and check on Vicky, then we can leave.'

CHAPTER TEN

The party was in full swing by the time they arrived at Bertie's West Vancouver waterfront apartment. As Courtenay preceded Graydon from the private lift into the luxurious penthouse suite, she felt as if she had just stepped into an exclusive night-club. The huge brightly lit lounge was wall-to-wall people, the women magnificently attired in colourful and dramatic designer outfits, the men an elegant foil in their dinner suits, and all of them balancing cocktails and canapés in their hands while shouting to each other over the deafening beat of a stereo. The air positively reeked of money, Courtenay decided—of French perfumes, trendy yuppie after-shaves, and fine imported wines.

Alanna had insisted that Courtenay borrow her mink stole, and as Graydon removed it from her shoulders and turned away to hand it to a uniformed attendant Courtenay saw Bertie emerge from the crowd and glide towards them.

She drew in a deep breath; if the other woman had hoped to be able to sneer at her appearance tonight she was going to be disappointed. Courtenay knew she had never looked lovelier—the velvet dress made her look svelte and sophisticated, its black silky texture the perfect showcase for her lustrous blonde hair, the creamy skin of her shoulders, and the swell of her breasts above the low-cut neckline. In addition, Graydon's kisses had done exactly what he'd wanted them to. . .and more! Her cheeks were flushed to the colour of delicate pink roses, and her eyes sparkled like brilliants.

155

There was no mistaking the anger glittering in Bertie's cat-yellow gaze as it raked over her. No mistaking the jealousy, or the spiteful compressing of the redhead's mocha-painted lips. But as Graydon finished talking with the attendant and turned round again Bertie's face swiftly became a warm and welcoming mask.

'Darling,' she purred, 'you *are* naughty! *Everyone's* here already, and you know I specially wanted you to come early. . .' Her bronze sequinned jumpsuit rippled in the light as she stood on tiptoe and brushed a kiss over his jaw. Then she took the bag he was carrying and peered inside. 'Good, you didn't forget the tapes. Brad's in charge of the music and he's been waiting for them. Will you just mingle? You do know everyone. I'll see you in a little while.' She glided away again without having once let her glance return to Courtenay.

'Bitch,' Courtenay whispered under her breath.

'What did you say?' Graydon frowned as he looked down at her.

For a moment Courtenay was tempted to pretend she'd said something else, but then she shrugged. 'I called her a bitch,' she said quietly. 'Her manners are atrocious.'

Graydon cupped her elbow with his hand and guided her along the periphery of the crowd towards the bar which was set up in the far corner. 'You don't like Bertie, do you?'

'No,' Courtenay said flatly, 'I don't.'

They reached the bar, and he said, 'What'll you have to drink?'

'I'll just have a Perrier, please.'

Graydon turned towards the barman. 'A Perrier and a Scotch on the rocks.'

It was obvious he didn't wish to discuss Bertie further. . .well, neither did she! Courtenay twisted round a little as he waited for the drinks, and, gripping her bag tightly, felt a surge of nervous excitement as her gaze darted over the crowd. Was he here, Patrick's friend. . .?

A group of five men were lounging around a grand piano just a few yards away to her right, and she stared at them intently. One she immediately eliminated as he was about six feet four, far taller than the man she remembered, a second she dismissed as he was unforgettably like Paul Newman. Frowning, she examined the third man. She could only see his profile, but he was of average build, with brown hair and regular features. She chewed her lip. Possible. . . But at that moment he turned to catch a passing waiter, and she exhaled a frustrated breath. He had a very noticeable birthmark on his right cheek.

'Checking out the action?' Graydon's cold voice in her ear made her jump, and with a startled 'Sorry?' Courtenay swivelled to face him. What had he said? Checking out the action?

He thrust her glass of Perrier at her. 'Can't wait, can you?' he said, his mouth twisting contemptuously. 'Which one do you fancy? Is it the Paul Newman lookalike? Would you like me to introduce you? Or do you prefer to make the first move yourself? His name's Dirk Mason. His wife, Penny, is in hospital, having their third child. . . But of course that won't stop *you*!'

Courtenay felt her throat tighten. Though she had physically wrenched herself away from him in her bedroom, she hadn't managed to detach herself emotionally, and the intimacy of their kisses had left an almost unbearable tension sizzling between them. Every cell in her body was exquisitely aware of his closeness—and she was in no doubt that he was as acutely aware of her. As they had come up in the lift, she had caught him looking at her, and when she had seen the dark

smouldering passion in his gaze the intensity of it had
made her feel as if the breath were being sucked from
her lungs.

Taking the glass from him, she shook her head.
'You're wrong,' she managed. 'I wasn't. . .checking out
the action, as you so crudely put it.'

'I was watching you in the bar mirror,' he said in a
low, harsh voice. 'If you weren't checking out the action,
why were you staring at those men in a way that could
only be described as. . .calculating?'

Their eyes locked, and, shrinking inside from the
angry challenge in his, she gripped the stem of her glass.
'I'm not denying I was staring at them,' she said. 'But
if I tell you why, you won't believe me, so what's
the——'

'Try me,' he snapped.

Courtenay sighed. 'You won't like what I'm
going——'

'For heaven's sake, get on with it!'

Taking a deep breath, Courtenay said, 'When Bertie
told me all her old skiing crowd would be here—the
crowd Patrick used to ski with—I thought. . .' She
hesitated.

'Thought what?'

'I thought that if I came to the party there was a
chance I might see Patrick's friend—the one who pretended to be a marriage commissioner at the wedding
ceremony I went through with Patrick.' She saw his
eyes flash angrily, but before he could say anything she
went on, 'You must have wondered why I agreed to
come with you—you know I can't stand Bertie. . .' She
looked up at him, prepared for a searing outburst, but
none came. Instead he said softly,

'And if you found this. . .friend of my brother's? What
then?'

'Why, I'd make him tell you the truth!' she said.

'And?'

Courtenay shook her head. 'That's all. I just want you to know you're wrong about me. I'm no home-wrecker.'

For a long moment he stared at her. Then he said abruptly, 'What does he look like, this. . .impostor?'

Why was he asking? She knew he didn't believe her. . . Defiantly she said, 'I have only a very vague picture of him in my mind—it was so long ago. He was about average height, I think, clean-shaven, sort of ordinary. . .'

The challenge in Graydon's eyes had hardened till it had the temper of steel. He took her arm, his fingers biting into the flesh. 'It shouldn't be too difficult. As you say, all the old ski crowd is here. I'll introduce you to every man in the room till you find the one you're looking for.

'And when you do,' he added mockingly, 'just tell me you'd like another Perrier. That will be the signal that you've found him; you can leave the rest to me.'

He isn't here.

The words Courtenay had spoken to Graydon after she'd finally met everyone at the party were still echoing miserably in her head a couple of hours later as she stood in Bertie's powder-room and stared unseeingly at her reflection in the mirror. She could almost feel Graydon's presence beside her, could almost feel again the pain shooting through her, as his grip had tightened savagely on her arm when their tour of the room was complete.

'No more Perrier, my love?'

His words had been like a stab-wound to her heart. He couldn't have hurt her more if he'd come right out with what he really meant. Now we've *proved* just what a little liar you are.

She had jerked her head up, expecting to see triumph in his eyes, but she'd caught him unawares, and as she saw the expression in the blue-green depths she felt shock jolt through her. Could that possibly have been *disappointment* she saw there? Had he been hoping she would find the man she'd been looking for?

Angrily Courtenay took her small brush from her bag, and ruthlessly attacked her long blonde hair. It must have been a trick of the light. She had blinked in astonishment, and when she'd opened her eyes again it was to see in Graydon's the mocking expression which was now so familiar to her. Her shoulders had slumped as she chastised herself for having let herself be fooled. . .even for a second. Why on *earth* would he have been disappointed that she hadn't been able to prove she was telling the truth about the fake marriage?

With a defeated sigh, she pushed her brush back into her bag and left the powder-room, grimacing as she heard the cacophonic sounds coming from the lounge. It was close to midnight, and the excitement was rising to fever-pitch. A few of the guests were dancing in a corner by the bar, and as Courtenay looked around for Graydon's familiar figure she finally spotted him there, with Bertie.

They weren't actually dancing, just swaying together in time to the music. Courtenay couldn't see Graydon's face, but she had a clear view of Bertie's. One cheek was nestled against her partner's chest, and her cat-yellow eyes were blissfully closed, her lips curved in an ecstatic smile.

Abruptly Courtenay turned away and walked back along the hallway. Why did she feel so miserable? It wasn't as if Graydon hadn't invited her to dance. He had. But she had refused. The way she was feeling about him tonight made her far too vulnerable; every time he had brushed against her or looked into her eyes she'd had to fight to overcome a desperate craving to drag him away into some quiet corner and beg him to make love to her. She had never before experienced desire so intense, so all-encompassing. It terrified her— not to mention twisting her stomach till it felt as if a whole pack of Girl Guides had been using it to perfect their knot-tying skills.

Not long after she and Graydon had arrived at the party he had shown her over the place, and she had been especially taken by a cosy TV room beyond which an adjoining sunroom looked out on the ocean. It had been unoccupied then. . . Courtenay prayed that it would still be so; it would provide her with a perfect place to hide and lick her wounds.

The TV room was in darkness save for the glow from a gas fire, but Courtenay could see that it was empty. Without turning on any lights, she skirted the furniture and pushed open the sliding doors leading to the sunroom. It was dark and shadowy, the large potted palms, ferns, and hanging baskets of trailing plants and flowers giving it a jungle atmosphere. It smelled like a flower shop, Courtenay thought, as she sank into the cushioned depths of a white wicker armchair and stared out into the purple-black night. A window was open, and she could faintly hear the steady roll of the ocean; it acted like a soothing lullaby, dulling her senses.

She had been so upset by Graydon's caustic 'No more Perrier, my love?' that she had reacted by saying harshly, 'No, no more Perrier. I'll have a Scotch, though. . .and make it a double.' Foolish of her, considering she had no head for alcohol. It always made her so sleepy. She hoped Graydon wouldn't come looking for her.

Graydon. . .

* * *

'There can never be anything between us,' Graydon's voice startled her. 'Not after what happened in the past.'

Courtenay jerked straight up in her chair. Wide-eyed, she stared around her, but there was no sign of the tall, wide-shouldered figure she had expected to find looming over her. But she'd heard his voice. . .so *clearly*! Dear lord, she must have dozed off, must have been dreaming. But it seemed so real, his voice so close——

'But darling, I love you! You must know that. I've never loved anyone else. And I know you loved me too.'

Courtenay felt as though someone had poured iced water down her spine. No, she hadn't been dreaming. That was Bertie's voice. . .and it came from the TV room. Suddenly she realised that the sunroom was no longer in shadowy darkness, but was half lit by the light now coming from the TV room. Swallowing, she realised she was listening to a private conversation. . .a *very* private conversation.

Her first impulse was to get up and hurry through to make her presence known. But in view of Bertie's pleading declaration of love for Graydon, how could she? How painfully embarrassing for the other woman to discover she'd been overheard. As Courtenay gripped the arms of her chair, torn, not knowing what to do, she heard Graydon say bitterly.

'You know damned well I loved you—good grief, when you accepted my proposal I was the happiest man alive. I wanted to shout the news from the top of Grouse Mountain! You were the one who insisted we keep our engagement secret——'

'Graydon, you know my parents would have hit the roof if I'd told them about you—about our. . .relationship. You had no money, you were just starting out——'

'Oh, you didn't *have* to tell them—they guessed! That was why they took you to England for the summer—to

try to break us up. . .and they succeeded. Your mother
must have been in seventh heaven when Sir Alex
Atherton took a fancy to you, even though he was more
than three times your age and had the IQ of a
gnat——'

'I was crazy, Gray, to have eloped with him! But
I liked nice things, and he dazzled me with
diamonds——'

'*I* could have dazzled you with diamonds,' Graydon
interrupted contemptuously, '*and* muffled you in mink—
if you'd waited for me as you promised! But Alex came
along, with his grand castle, and all his millions. . .'

'Don't look at me like that, darling. I can't bear it!'

Graydon went on as if he hadn't heard her. 'I have to
thank you, though, Bertie, for teaching me a very
important lesson.'

'A lesson? What lesson?'

'Money is power. Up till that time, I'd measured
success by a different yardstick, but when I found out
how Alex Atherton had bought you I swore I'd spend
my life accumulating a fortune, so that I'd possess the
power that goes along with——'

'Good lord, you've changed, Graydon! You've
become so hard——'

'You've changed too,' he broke in harshly. 'I don't
know you any more. Or maybe you were always like
this, but I just didn't see it.'

'It's that woman, isn't it?' Bertie's tone was suddenly
vicious. 'She's the one who's come between us, the one
who's spoiled everything. Patrick's. . .whore!'

For a moment Courtenay sat stunned, unable to
believe what she had just heard. Then rage surged up
inside her with such force that it propelled her from her
chair. No way was she going to just sit there and let
Roberta Atherton insult her. And to think she'd stayed
hidden so as not to cause the woman embarrassment!

She stumbled to the doorway of the TV room, blood rushing in her ears with the sound of a waterfall, and stared at the scene before her. Graydon was gripping Bertie's shoulders, his expression thunderous, and the redhead's lipsticked mouth hung slackly open as she cringed from him.

Courtenay's heart drummed with such force that she wondered that they hadn't heard it. Taking a deep, shuddering breath in a vain attempt to calm herself, she stepped forward. 'Excuse me. . .'

Bertie gasped with surprise, then fury blazed to life in her yellow cat's eyes as she saw Courtenay. Graydon seemed to freeze for a second, then, dropping his hands from Bertie's shoulders with an exclamation of disgust, he focused his attention on Courtenay.

'I wondered where you'd got to. I didn't realise there was anyone in the sunroom.' He frowned, taking a step towards her. 'Why didn't you make your presence known earlier?'

'I dozed off—not enough Perrier, too much Scotch,' Courtenay said sarcastically. Then, directing her icy gaze at Bertie, she said in arctic tones, 'I'd like to set the record straight. I have *never* been—and never will be—anyone's whore. If anyone deserves that ugly title, it's yourself. My only mistake was being taken in by sweet words and promises; *you*, according to what I heard you say a moment ago, sold yourself for a handful of diamonds!'

While she was talking, Courtenay had been supported by the blind rage which held her in its grip. Now she felt reaction set in. Her head began to spin dizzily, and she must have begun to sway, because all of a sudden Graydon was by her side, his arm around her.

'Are you all right?'

The concern in his voice reminded her of the kindness he had shown her when she'd spilled the coffee on

herself. . .the kindness he would have shown to anyone
who had been hurt. But when he gently brushed back a
few strands of her hair that had become disarrayed
while she slept she felt her pulse-rate quicken. He had
never treated her quite so tenderly before—never
treated her in a way that seemed to indicate that he
cared for her. When he had put his arm round her, his
jacket had swung open, and now he pulled her close—
far closer than was necessary, and she could feel the
hard muscles of his chest, the drumming of his heart
against her bare shoulder. What was going on? she
wondered dizzily. What had happened to cause his
change of attitude? He was acting as if they were
lovers. . .

'Yes,' she managed to whisper. 'I'm fine. But I'd like
to go home.'

Home. When had she begun to think of Seacliffe as
home. Had he noticed the little slip? Involuntarily she
raised her head, and the burning intensity of his gaze as
it locked with hers sent a series of shock waves rippling
through her. Oh, yes, he had noticed. Courtenay felt
her lower lip tremble. She was aware of him as she had
never been aware of him before. Aware of the beautiful
green flecks in his eyes, aware of the slight roughness of
his fingertips as he openly caressed her forearm, aware
of the intoxicating male scent from his hair and skin. . .

'You're doing it again,' he breathed, and Courtenay
felt as if her cheeks were suddenly aflame. She knew
what he meant. She looked as if she was waiting for him
to kiss her——

Bertie's coarse laugh shattered the tension between
them, and, controlling a shudder, Courtenay dragged
her gaze from Graydon's. The redhead's face was con-
torted with anger. 'Oh, Graydon, you damned fool!' she
shrilled. 'Are you blind? Can't you see through that
sweet, innocent façade? Can't you see her for the cheap

slut that she is? Patrick was too smart to be trapped—
he took what he wanted and——'

'We're leaving, Bertie,' Graydon's voice cut through
her words like a whiplash, 'before I do something no
man should do to a woman!'

'But you can't!' Bertie gaped at him disbelievingly.
'You can't leave so early—what will everybody think?'

Graydon tightened his grip around Courtenay's
shoulders, and as he swept her from the room she had
to half run to keep up with his long stride. She knew
people were staring as they jostled their way through
the crowd towards the entrance hall, but it was as if
they were in a different world.

She barely noticed that Graydon had placed the stole
around her shoulders, and as they descended in the lift
and crossed the foyer to the front door of the building
she felt as if she was moving in the midst of a thick grey
fog and no longer knew where she was going.

She shivered as they walked out to the parking area,
not sure whether her body was reacting to the cold or to
Graydon's disturbing touch on her bare skin. The air
was tangy and fresh, and she filled her lungs with it,
hoping in vain that it would clear her head.

A cab was drawing up at the kerb a few yards away,
but she paid no attention to the man who alighted till
she heard Graydon say in a frustrated tone, 'Oh, damn,
it's Bertie's brother!' He muttered something unintelli-
gible under his breath as the bearded figure glanced
round.

'Graydon Winter!' The newcomer's green eyes
gleamed in recognition as he closed the space between
them and shook hands with Graydon. 'Long time no
see, old buddy.' He glanced at Courtenay and did a
double-take. 'Hey, introduce me to your friend—the
first decent-looking woman I've seen since I got out of
the jungle!'

'Courtenay,' Graydon's voice was strained, 'this is John Andrews, Bertie's brother—the anthropologist I told you about. He's been down in the Amazon for the past six months, living in a shack miles from civilization. . .'

Courtenay barely heard what Graydon was saying. She was staring at Bertie's brother, at this John Andrews, at his green eyes, his straight brown hair, at the rather weak mouth that was almost hidden by the bushy ginger beard. Her heart began thumping like a jack-hammer against her ribcage.

'When did you grow your beard?' she asked faintly.

A puzzled look flitted across the long green eyes. 'My beard? Heavens, I've had this beard for. . .must be close to nine years now.'

Courtenay felt her legs wobble as she transferred her gaze from Bertie's brother to the tall figure standing beside her. In some distant part of her mind it registered that in the light slanting down from the street-lamp his face had suddenly become as deathly pale as a corpse.

'Graydon——' she hardly recognised her own voice, '—I believe I'm ready to have that second glass of Perrier now.'

Courtenay sat huddled in the back of the cab as it swished its way along Marine Drive towards Seacliffe. She barely knew how she'd landed there—it certainly hadn't been of her own volition, but she had been too shattered to think for herself. With a harsh shout, Graydon had hailed the driver as he was pulling away from the kerb, and, bundling her inside, had tugged a twenty-dollar bill from his wallet and thrust it into her hand.

'I'll see you at home. Wait up for me; this won't take long.'

The last thing she remembered seeing was the savage

fury glittering in his eyes as he turned to face Bertie's brother.

'This where you wanna go, lady?'

Courtenay jumped. Peering out of the window, she said unsteadily, 'Oh. . .yes. Thank you.' She reached across and gave him the money Graydon had thrust at her. 'Keep the change. . .and,' she added as she opened the car door, 'have a good new year.'

Livvy and her sister Jan were coming down the stairs as she walked into the hall. Before she could ask how Vicky was, Jan said reassuringly, 'We've just checked her. She's sound asleep—went out like a light around nine, and hasn't surfaced since.'

Livvy smiled. 'Wheeler has a cottage on the grounds—he's invited us for a drink. Mrs Winter said it'd be all right if I went out after you got back. There's a tray with some cookies and a Thermos of freshly brewed coffee in the drawing-room.'

'Thanks, Livvy. I hope you both have a good time at Wheeler's party.'

'Good night—and a Happy New Year,' the sisters chorused as they hurried away.

Courtenay slipped off her high-heeled sandals and, carrying them in her hand, tiptoed upstairs in her nyloned feet. Weariness shrouded her, and as she quietly opened Vicky's door and saw her daughter's fragile little body curled up in bed she felt a painful constriction of her throat. Slumping against the doorframe, she stared mindlessly into the dimly lit room.

How could her life have become so confused, so difficult? Less than two weeks ago she had been happy and contented with her world—a world that comprised Vicky and herself. And a world of which she was in charge.

But ever since Graydon Winter had entered that world she had felt as if she were being sucked under by a powerful whirlpool—a whirlpool of desire. The only thing that had saved her from being drowned completely was her knowledge that he despised her. But he no longer had any reason to do so.

There was no doubt he'd get the whole story out of John; the anthropologist would be no match for him. . .so how would he treat her when he returned to Seacliffe? How would he treat her, knowing he had been wrong about the kind of woman she was?

She took a deep breath and pushed herself from the doorframe. He said he wouldn't take long. She would go downstairs to the drawing-room and wait for him.

Every second, she knew, would seem like an eternity.

Graydon came home just as the old year ended and the new year began. Courtenay didn't hear the Mercedes purr into the forecourt, or the front door open, because of the resounding clap of fireworks in the distance. For a fraction of a second she thought it was thunder. Then as the din of car horns stridently jarred the air from closer at hand she realised the sounds she was hearing were sounds of celebration. Moving to the window, she pulled back the curtains. The sky across the inlet was a palette of reds, yellows, greens as Catherine wheels and rockets painted the darkness with vivid colour.

The creaking of a floorboard behind her made her jerk her head round, and she felt her heartbeats give an erratic stagger as she saw Graydon standing just inside the door. The fabric of the curtains slipped from her suddenly nerveless fingers as she saw how white and haggard he looked, his black hair tousled back from his brow, as if he'd been dragging his fingers through it over and over.

She thought he was never going to move; even wondered if he was going to look at her like that forever, his eyes dark with despair, his mouth twisted bleakly.

But finally he pushed the door slowly shut and walked forward, stopping several feet away from her.

'John told me the whole story.' His voice had the rough texture of gravel being ground through a metal mesh. 'Apparently he owed Patrick a favour, so when my brother confessed that he'd met a young blonde virgin who didn't believe in pre-marital sex, and he'd go mad if he couldn't have her, John agreed to——' He dragged a hand over suddenly glistening eyes, then, shaking his head, he turned away from her and walked to the hearth, where he stood with his back to her, every taut line in his bearing telling of his agony.

'You don't have to say any more,' Courtenay said faintly. 'I don't want to hear. It's all in the past.' She ran her right hand distractedly up and down her left arm. 'I'm sorry.'

'*You're* sorry?' He looked round briefly, and the pain in his eyes made her heart ache. 'What in the name of heaven have *you* got to be sorry about?'

She gestured helplessly. 'You believed in your brother. It must be. . .hard for you to accept that he wasn't the man you thought he was.'

Graydon looked away from her again, and, gripping the edge of the mantelpiece, leaned forward, head bent. For a long moment he didn't speak. And then at last, in a voice so low that she could barely hear it, he murmured, 'Yes, that's hard. But it's harder by far for me to accept the way I've treated you. Dear God!' He whirled round to face her, his eyes dark with anguish. 'No wonder you didn't want to come to Seacliffe with me—no wonder you don't want anything to do with the Winter family! We've all treated you abominably, unforgivably. Alanna's going to be devastated when I tell her what we've done——'

'Oh, no!' Involuntarily, Courtenay took a step

towards him. 'You mustn't tell her. She needn't ever find out——'

'You really think that of me?' He asked, his voice incredulous. 'That I'd let my mother go on believing you're a. . .'

'A whore?' Courtenay met his gaze evenly. 'I'd rather have her think that of me than have you hurt her. She's suffered so much already——'

'The truth has to be told.' He met her gaze, and she saw him shake his head as if he found it impossible to believe what he had just heard. 'You would actually do that? Sacrifice yourself in that way?'

Courtenay just looked at him, her answer in her eyes.

Graydon dragged a hand exhaustedly across his brow. 'Oh, lord, how could I have been so wrong about you?' He sounded utterly defeated. 'Yes, it *will* be distressing for Alanna, but the alternative is unthinkable.' Taking a deep breath, he gestured towards one of the armchairs. 'Will you sit down? I want to hear your story—if you're still interested in telling it, that is. I wouldn't blame you if——'

'No,' Courtenay said, 'I'll tell you what happened.' She sat down, but though he moved to the opposite side of the hearth he didn't take a seat. Instead he stood, feet slightly apart, his hands hanging loosely at his sides, and looked down at her, waiting.

'After I graduated from high school,' she began quietly, 'I found a job at the Snowpeak Hotel in Whistler—in the office. On nice days, I often sat on a bench in a nearby park during my lunch-hour. One day, while I was sitting there in the sun, I heard a sound, and when I glanced up it was to find someone—a man—taking a picture of me.'

She saw a nerve flicker in Graydon's cheek, and a strangely haunted look appear briefly in his eyes. Swallowing, she went on, 'That's where I met Patrick, not in any bar.' She grimaced, and gave a mirthless laugh. 'I was only seventeen, so I wouldn't have been served in a——'

'*Seventeen*?' There was no mistaking the surprise in his voice—and the horror. 'You were just seventeen? My God, that makes what Patrick did even more despicable. . .' He didn't say anything for a long moment, but his eyes blazed with anger. Finally he went on, 'You're twenty-seven now?'

'Twenty-eight.'

'A very mature twenty-eight.'

'I grew up fast, after Patrick informed me our relationship was over. The doctor had just that morning told me I was pregnant, and I'd been waiting for Patrick to come home to share the news——'

'Home?'

'I had a room in one of the houses belonging to the hotel company. He told me he had something to tell me, so I hugged my own news to myself, waiting for him to tell his first. But when I found out what he wanted to say—that he was married and our wedding had been a fake, and he didn't want to see me again——'

'You decided to keep the news of your pregnancy to yourself.'

The fire sparked and hissed, the only sound breaking the silence between them. A silence that was heavy with deep emotion and unspoken words. Finally, Courtenay could bear the tension no longer, and she pushed herself up from her chair.

'It's been a long day,' she said, smoothing down the black velvet dress. 'I'm going to bed.' As she turned to leave, she hesitated. 'Oh, there's just one thing. . .'

'What's that?'

'You found out the reason I wanted to go to Bertie's party, but you said you had a reason for taking me there. Will you tell me what your reason was? I'd like to know.'

She saw a muscle twitch at the base of his throat. Jerkily he ripped open his red bow-tie and loosened the collar of his white shirt. 'I was hoping you'd forgotten about that,' he said tersely. 'But since we're being honest with each other, yes, I'll tell you my reason for taking you to the party.'

Courtenay heard the self-contempt lacing his voice, and with a hissed, indrawn breath she wrapped her arms around herself protectively, waiting for the hurt that she knew was to come.

'I invited you to go with me,' he went on, 'because I wanted Bertie to think there was something between us. Ever since her husband's death, she'd been more than hinting that we should take up where we left off. I thought the most effective way of getting the message across that there was no chance of that ever happening was to——'

'Was to use me,' Courtenay finished dully. She felt a smarting behind her eyelids and her throat tightened till it was almost too painful to swallow. 'I should have guessed,' she said, her voice husky with tears. 'Par for the Winter course.'

She turned and stumbled towards the door. But before she reached it Graydon had caught up with her. He gripped her shoulders and spun her round.

'Dear heavens. . .' his voice was filled with torment '. . . I'm sorry, Courtenay.'

She looked up into his eyes, and saw the remorse glimmering there. Unable to speak for the misery overwhelming her, she slid from under his grasp and made for the door.

This time he didn't try to stop her.

CHAPTER ELEVEN

COURTENAY was relieved to find that Graydon had
gone to the office by the time she got up next morning.
After taking a breakfast tray to Vicky, she went back to
the kitchen for a mug of coffee, the only bright spot in
her day being that her daughter was well and truly on
the mend.

She chatted for a few minutes with Livvy, and when
she walked back to the hall with the steaming mug of
coffee in her hand she saw Alanna poking about among
the pots of paint and rolls of wallpaper.

She cleared her throat. 'Happy New Year, Mrs
Winter.'

'Ah. . .good morning—and Happy New Year to you
too.' The older woman's voice was taut. 'I. . . I was
waiting for you. I'd like to speak with you. Do you have
a moment?'

Courtenay felt a twinge of apprehension as she
noticed Alanna's red-rimmed eyes; it was obvious that
she had been weeping. 'I was going back upstairs to sit
with Vicky,' she said quietly, 'but. . .yes, of course I
have a moment.'

They walked into the drawing-room, and Alanna
gestured to Courtenay to sit down in one of the wing
chairs. The fire had just been lit, and it crackled noisily
as the flames licked the dry kindlers and logs. Alanna
sank down into the chair opposite, her gaze falling to
the yellow tongues darting up the chimney.

Courtenay waited for her to speak, but the seconds
stretched out between them. She took a few sips of her
coffee, then, just as she decided she must start a

conversation in order to break the tension, Alanna turned to her.

'Graydon has told me *everything*,' the older woman said unsteadily. 'The whole wretched story of how Patrick tricked you and seduced you. From the bottom of my heart, I want to beg your forgiveness for the abominable way I've treated you. I've never felt so ashamed in my life. You were a guest in my home, and my behaviour has been appalling.'

So Graydon had lost no time in setting things straight. Courtenay had to admire him for that. . .it must have been an unpleasant task. 'You only knew what Graydon told you when he brought us here,' Courtenay said gently. 'You had no way of knowing it wasn't the truth.'

'I should have!' Alanna's brows lowered fiercely. 'I should have followed my own instincts. I've always prided myself on being a good judge of character. The more I saw of you, the more puzzled I found myself— you didn't seem to fit the picture Graydon had painted of you. And then on Christmas morning when you came running upstairs you looked so dreadfully unhappy that I found myself wanting to knock on your bedroom door and ask what was wrong. I guessed Bertie Atherton had been rude to you.' She sighed. 'I went on downstairs, but I couldn't forget the expression of despair in your eyes. It haunted me. Now I bitterly regret not having made that move.'

Courtenay felt her heart ache for Alanna—but she also felt a small glow of hope. Could they now be friends, something that had been impossible before? 'Your apology is accepted. Let's put the past behind us and——'

Alanna shook her head. 'First, there's something else I must say. Graydon told me you pleaded with him to keep the truth from me, because you were afraid I'd be hurt.' There was a suspicion of tears in the faded blue eyes. 'You were right—it was exceedingly painful for me to accept what Patrick had done. But the pain was softened by the knowledge of your caring. How very generous of you to have wanted to spare me in that way—I don't think I've ever met anyone with such a lovely nature. Is it too much to hope that you'll let me consider you one of the family from now on? Too much to hope that you'll stay on with us here at Seacliffe?'

One of the family. Courtenay had a fleeting image of her father's contemptuous expression when he'd told her he never wanted to see her again. Now she was being given the opportunity to be part of another family—something she had never hoped for in her wildest dreams. She felt drawn to Alanna, in the way she would surely have been drawn to her own mother.

'Mrs Winter——'

'Do call me Alanna, dear. *All* my friends do.'

Courtenay smiled shakily. 'Alanna, you're Vicky's grandmother, and I'd like very much for us both to be part of your family. But I'm afraid I still plan on going back to Millar's Lake in a few days. That's our home— mine and Vicky's. My independence is very important to me.' She bit her lip as she saw Alanna's face fall, and she went on quickly, 'Perhaps I can find a bigger apartment, then Wheeler could drive you up any time you wanted to visit. And if Vicky wants to visit you during her school holidays—as I'm sure she will!—then Wheeler could come up for her. I certainly would have no objection to that.'

'Wheeler. . .' Alanna murmured the chauffeur's name in an absent tone, as if she was thinking of something else entirely. For a long moment she looked at Courtenay without talking. Her eyes no longer seemed faded. . .in fact, Courtenay thought as she found herself wanting to wriggle uncomfortably under the sharp scrutiny; they seemed to be looking right into her and reading her innermost thoughts. How utterly ridiculous!

Then at last Alanna made a sound—a small hiss, as she drew in her breath sharply. 'Oh, my dear, how could I have been so blind? It's Graydon, isn't it? That's the reason you won't stay on here, the reason you're so determined to go home. You've fallen in love with him!'

Courtenay jumped up so quickly that a few drops of coffee spilled on the carpet. Confusedly, she placed her mug on the hearth, and, tugging a tissue from the pocket of her jeans, bent to rub the spots away. She was thankful for the excuse to hide her face from the other woman; she could feel it flaming like a furnace. 'Oh, no,' she said in a muffled voice, as she kept rubbing relentlessly though the coffee spots had disappeared. 'You're mistaken.'

'Am I?' Alanna had got to her feet. 'Then why,' she asked quietly, 'are you arranging the future so that you need never see him again? Why must it be *Wheeler* who drives me to Millar's Lake, why must it be *Wheeler* who drives there to collect Vicky? Why not. . . *Graydon*?'

Courtenay threw the crumpled tissue into the fire and finally—reluctantly—straightened. 'I. . .it's just that he's such a busy man, and I don't want to inconvenience him. . .'

But as she met Alanna's level gaze, the words trailed away, unconvincing even in her own ears. Dismay coursed through her as she absorbed the full impact of what the other woman had just said. Was it possible? Had she fallen in love with Graydon? Had she been so blinded by the searing desire that blazed between them that she hadn't seen what was happening? The room seemed to sway around her, and blindly she grasped the edge of the mantelpiece for support as she faced the shattering truth. Yes, Alanna was right. She had fallen in love.

But the man to whom she had so unknowingly, so completely given her heart was a man who didn't want it.

Oh, dear heavens. . .he must *never* find out.

'Please don't tell him,' she begged, tears choking her words. 'I couldn't face him if he knew.'

'Of course I won't.' Alanna's voice was filled with compassion. 'Of course I won't. It would be unbearably embarrassing for you. You see, Graydon was betrayed very badly by someone when he was younger—he never confided in me who the woman was, but I know the affair destroyed his trust in women. He swore then that he would never marry.' Alanna shook her head sadly. 'And once my son makes up his mind about something nothing in the whole wide world will make him change it.'

She took Courtenay's cold hands in hers and held them. 'Don't worry, my dear, your secret is safe with me.'

Yes, Courtenay thought as she slumped back in her chair again, she knew her secret *would* be safe with Alanna. But the knowledge did little to assuage the pain that was tearing her heart.

The rest of the morning crept by at a snail's pace. Courtenay played Fly-Trap with Vicky, the game she'd given her for Christmas, but her mind wasn't on it. All she could think of was Graydon, and the sheer impossibility of the days that lay ahead before she could leave Seacliffe.

Vicky fell asleep around one-thirty, and before going down for her own nap Alanna patted Courtenay's arm and suggested she should go for a walk.

'You look so tired, and it's lovely out—the exercise will do you a world of good. I've told Livvy to listen for Victoria in case she wakens before you get back.'

Alanna was right, Courtenay thought a few minutes later as she examined her reflection in the bathroom mirror. She *did* look tired—and no wonder, for she had barely slept all night. Neither, she knew, had Graydon; she had heard him pacing back and forth in his bedroom in the small hours, as if he was trying to work out some insoluble problem.

With a heavy sigh she scraped her hair into a ponytail, and, after securing it with a white ribbon, she changed from the skirt she'd been wearing into a pair of jeans, and put on a navy crewneck sweater over her white cotton blouse. She looked, she decided wryly, like a well-scrubbed, carefree teenager—but only on the surface. She knew that anyone who cared to look deeply into her eyes would see the shadow of her pain.

She ran downstairs, slipping on her trainers before going out. As she closed the front door behind her, a robin hopped from the drive to the bare branch of a nearby maple tree. She paused, lifting a hand to her forehead to shield her gaze from the sun, and watched the bird's perky progress.

It was a gorgeous afternoon, the warm breeze bringing to her nostrils the scent of woodsmoke mingled with the seaweedy tang from the shore. She closed her eyes, trying to concentrate on the perfection of the day, but that very perfection seemed only to make more poignant the emptiness of her life as it stretched ahead of her—a life without Graydon. It hardly seemed ppossible that only a week or two ago she had thought she didn't need anyone but Vicky; how very wrong she had been!

The purr of an approaching vehicle made her eyes fly open, and to her dismay she saw the Mercedes come round the corner of the drive. The wheels crunched on the gravel as it pulled to a stop just yards from where she stood. She felt as if a cloud had covered the bright sun. Please, she prayed, let it be Wheeler. . .

But her prayer wasn't answered.

As Graydon uncoiled his long body from the driver's seat she fought back an almost overwhelming urge to scuttle away into the rhododendron bushes and hide. Instead, taking a deep breath, she slid her hands into the back pockets of her jeans and waited as he walked towards her.

He was wearing a dark business suit and a silver-grey shirt. As the breeze caught his red tie, drawing Courtenay's attention to his muscular chest, she found herself remembering how Krystle had raved about him that day in the Mom's Own office. 'Tall, dark, and absolutely devastating. He has the sexiest scowl, and jet black hair, a Palm Springs tan, eyes the colour of peacock feathers. . .' Courtenay shivered as she also recalled what she herself had said a moment or two later. 'You know I'm not interested in men.'

'Where are you going?' Graydon's abrupt question broke into her thoughts.

She swallowed to relieve the tightness in her throat, and, turning her head from him, gestured towards the waterfront. 'Your mother tells me it's possible to walk along the beach for a mile or so. I thought I'd get a breath of fresh air while Vicky's sleeping.'

'I looked in on her this morning before I went out. She seemed a lot better.'

'Yes, she's coming along well.' The silence between them stretched awkwardly, and, to fill it, Courtenay said, 'She told me you'd gone to the office. Don't you ever take a break? After all, this *is* a holiday.'

'I did go to the office, but I wasn't working.' Graydon looked beyond her, to where the sea sparkled in the winter sunshine. 'I had some thinking to do.'

'I heard you pacing in your room, way after midnight——' Courtenay halted. Why had she said that? She hadn't meant to let him know she had heard him.

'Did I disturb you?' He frowned.

'No, I was awake too. I. . .hope you came up with whatever answers you were looking for.'

'Yes,' he murmured. 'Yes, I believe I did.'

She had never noticed before just how hawkish his features were, but now, as he stared out to sea, she realised how very strong his profile was, how very determined. The rugged strength of a man who knew his own mind. . .

What was it Alanna had said? 'Once my son makes up his mind about something, nothing in the whole world will make him change it?' Despair spiralled through her.

'Unless you have any objection, of course?'

Courtenay blinked, and looked at him. 'Sorry,' she muttered, 'I didn't catch. . .?'

His eyes reflected the blue of the sky as he met her questioning gaze. 'I said I thought I'd stretch my legs too, if you don't mind my joining you?'

'Oh. . . Sure.' Courtenay lifted her shoulders in a shrug, a shrug that belied the sudden thudding of her heart against her ribcage.

The sand was damp but firm, and the walking was easy. Gigantic weathered logs littered the shore, but they weren't in the way, as they lay horizontal to the shoreline. There was no one else on the long stretch of beach, save for a teenage girl away up ahead, who was throwing pieces of driftwood for her dog to retrieve.

'I phoned Alanna after lunch.' Graydon's voice broke into her thoughts. 'She said you and she had talked. I don't know what miracle you wrought, but she told me—rather smugly—that she's going to phone the painters next week and ask them to get on with the front hall.'

'Oh, that's wonderful!' Courtenay's eyes sparkled. 'Such a good sign.'

'I think so too.'

'So I can go back to Millar's Lake as soon as Vicky is well enough to travel.'

'You still plan to leave?' His voice was stiff.

'Yes,' Courtenay said evenly. 'I still plan to leave.'

He kicked a small rock out of his path. 'I'll drive you back, then.'

'Oh, that's not necessary!' To sit in a car with him, at such close quarters for so many hours, would be sheer torture—she'd rather be stretched out on a bed of nails with a sword dangling over her from a thread. 'We'll take the bus.'

'Wheeler will drive you.' This time his tone brooked no argument.

They walked for a few minutes before he spoke again. 'I'll get in touch with Ketterton tomorrow. You'll be reinstated in your job. I'll talk to him about arranging to have you adequately reimbursed by the company for——'

'No.' Courtenay's voice was hard. 'No, I won't take any money from you—ever. So please don't do that. All I want to do is go back home, and have everything the way it was before. Oh, I know that's not quite possible, but——'

'You still hate me, don't you?' The statement was harshly uttered.

Courtenay opened her mouth to protest, but closed it again quickly. Wouldn't it be for the best if he believed that? If he believed that she couldn't stand the sight of him? That way, she need never see him again. He would make sure that Wheeler was the one who transported Vicky whenever she went to Seacliffe for her holidays.

Their steps had slowed while they'd been talking; now Courtenay turned from him so that he wouldn't see the glint of tears in her eyes. She had thought Patrick had broken her heart; she knew now that what she had felt for him had been only a teenage infatuation, a pale, shallow imitation of the real thing. What she felt for Graydon was love, love of the everlasting kind. She knew that she would never fall in love again. This was the only man for her.

But he didn't love her; and she wouldn't settle for an affair. They both deserved better than that.

She smelled his male scent a second before he grasped her shoulders and turned her round. Furiously blinking away her tears before he could see them, she stared up at him, feeling a sob catch in her throat as she saw the haunted look in his beautiful eyes.

He dropped his hands, and stepped back a little so that they weren't touching. 'You've never asked me how I found out Patrick had a child,' he said, his voice thick with emotion.

Courtenay stared at him, confusion dulling her mind. 'No,' she said slowly, 'I never did. I just assumed. . .' Her words trailed away. 'I was going to say I just assumed that after Patrick's death it occurred to you that his affair might have resulted in a child, and with Beth no longer around to be hurt any more, you hired a private investigator to check the idea out.'

He looked along the beach, at the girl and the dog. He didn't speak for a few moments, then he said jerkily, 'Let's sit down.'

There was a huge log directly in front of them, and Courtenay swung one leg over it and then the other, and, after flicking away some grains of sand, she sat down.

Graydon took a seat on the log, a couple of feet away from her. 'No,' he said. 'The possibility that there might be a child had never occurred to me.'

Courtenay looked at him in astonishment. 'Then why did you come looking for me?' A chilling idea rippled through her mind. 'Did you want to get some sort of. . .*revenge?*'

'Revenge?' He stared out to sea for such a long time that she began to wonder if he was going to say any more. But then at last he said in a self-derisive tone, 'No, not revenge.' After another long silence he gave a weary sigh. Reaching into the hip pocket of his trousers, he extricated a wallet, and Courtenay watched with a puzzled frown as he ran his thumb over the expensive leather.

'The answer is in here,' he said slowly, as if he could hardly bear to bring the words out. 'I never thought I'd show this to anyone. . .least of all you. But I don't want there to be any more secrets. . .between us.'

Courtenay shivered as the breeze gusted across her face. 'What is it?'

He held out the wallet. 'Open it. You'll see for yourself.'

Her hands felt cold. She rubbed them together, and looked up at him, bewilderment obvious.

'Open it,' Graydon repeated tonelessly.

He made sure their fingers didn't touch as she took the wallet. As he had done, she rubbed a thumb over the fine leather, putting off the moment when she'd have to look inside. What could it be? What could have led him to search her out? Search *her* out—not Vicky.

Slowly she opened the wallet. The first thing she saw was a photo, behind a plastic window. An old photo, dog-eared, slightly faded——

Her stomach muscles clenched convulsively as she stared at it disbelievingly. It was a photo of herself—the one Patrick had taken the day they met. She recalled the first words he had ever spoken to her. . .

'Sorry. . .' His lips had curved in a rueful, charming grin. 'I just couldn't resist. You're the sexiest female I've ever seen in my life!'

Lips parted, she stared at Graydon. 'Where did you get this?' she breathed.

'I found it in a locked drawer when I was clearing out Patrick's office after he died.'

'But why did you keep it?' she asked. An answer flitted into her brain, an answer she didn't want to hear. An answer she prayed she wouldn't hear.

The answer he gave her anyway. 'I kept it because I thought you were the sexiest female I'd ever seen in my life.'

Courtenay looked at him disbelievingly, feeling as if the world had turned on its axis and had, in a split second, come full circle. Her body seemed to have become weightless. And then the moment passed, and, with a choking cry, she got up, hardly noticing that the wallet dropped on to the sand as she ran to the water's edge. She started out at the horizon, not seeing a thing through the tears blurring her eyes. She didn't hear Graydon coming up behind her, but she knew he was there because she could feel his warm breath ruffling the hair at her nape. Still he didn't touch her.

She shook her head despairingly. 'You wanted me. . .' Tears clogged her throat. 'You wanted me—*wanted my body*—just the way Patrick did. You're just like him. . .Oh, I can't bear it!'

'Look at me, Courtenay.'

It was no longer important that she hide her tears from him. Pressing her palms to her temples in a vain effort to rid herself of a sudden painful throbbing, she whirled round, but her angry words died in her throat as she saw the tortured look in his eyes. Panting a little, she stood there, arms raised, as if frozen.

'I became obsessed with your image,' he said in an anguished voice. 'I could think of nothing else, day or night. Yes, I hired a detective to track you down, but not because it even entered my head that you might have a child of Patrick's, but *because I wanted you*. Yes, you're right. . . I wanted you, just as Patrick wanted you.'

Courtenay felt as if he had taken her broken heart and crushed it into a million tiny pieces. How could she have let herself fall in love with this man? He was no better than his brother.

'When the private investigator eventually found you, and told me you had a child, I asked him to send me a photo. When I saw how like Patrick your daughter was. . .' He shook his head helplessly. 'Alanna's depression was a heaven-sent excuse to bring you down here, to get you into my home. I even fooled myself for a while into believing that it was really for Alanna's sake, because she wanted a grandchild, that I went to the lengths I did. But of course it wasn't. It was you I wanted. And I still want you.'

With a little sob, Courtenay dropped her hands and began to walk away from him. She didn't have to listen to this. Listen to him saying——'

'But now I want more——' he was right behind her, but still he made no attempt to touch her '—more than just the beautiful, sexy blonde in the picture. I want the real Courtenay—the warm, vulnerable, unselfish woman I've fallen in love with. I want to marry her, I want to live with her for the rest of my life. . .'

Hardly believing what she was hearing, Courtenay halted. But she couldn't turn round. If she did, she might find no one there, might find she was hallucinating, imagining things she wanted to hear.

'Courtenay. . .'

Taking in a deep breath, she finally managed to face him again, and, clasping her arms around herself, stared up at him unwaveringly as she waited for him to go on.

'I know that Patrick shattered your trust in men.' His dark-fringed eyes were filled with pain and regret. 'But

I hope he didn't destroy it completely. I hope it can be rebuilt. I know I can't expect that to happen overnight—and perhaps it's better that way, because I want to earn that trust; I *need* to earn it. . .and,' a muscle twitched in his determinedly set jaw, 'I *plan* to earn it, no matter how long it takes. Even if it takes forever.'

How? Courtenay wanted to ask, but she couldn't get the word out. Graydon answered her anyway.

'I'm going to court you, the way you deserve to be courted, the way you've never been courted. And to do that we have to start at the beginning again. We have to pretend we're strangers, a man and a woman who have never met before.' He squared his shoulders and said with a simple conviction that set Courtenay's heart spinning, 'I'm going to make you love me.'

But you don't need to, she cried silently, I'm already in love with you.

He surely read something of her response in her eyes, for he smiled. It was, Courtenay realised, the first real smile he had ever sent her way—and the love, the commitment in his expression removed any last doubts that might have been lingering in her heart. She suddenly felt as if she were on a brightly coloured balloon, floating heavenwards.

'I guess,' he murmured in a husky voice, 'there's no better time and place to start than right now and right here.'

Courtenay had her back to the sun, yet she felt as if it was blinding her. She could hear the sucking sound as the wavelets retreated down the sand, she could hear the cry of a seagull overhead. And she could hear, above all, the chorus of angels singing in her heart. She smiled back at him, and, as she did, she heard his sharply indrawn breath, and could have sworn she saw him tremble.

But when he held out his hand and took hers, it was firm and warm and strong.

'Hi,' he said, 'I'd like to introduce myself.' He held her fingers only briefly. 'My name's Graydon Winter. I live in that house among the pines. I'm financially secure and my mother thinks I'm a pretty nice guy.'

Courtenay thought she wasn't going to be able to answer, happiness had brought such an aching lump to her throat. But at last she managed to swallow it away.

'Courtenay West.' Her voice was tremulous, but it held a hint of laughter. 'Single mother, with a nine-year-old daughter. I'm financially insecure, and the place I call home is a rather shabby basement flat in Millar's Lake.'

'Millar's Lake? Is that a nice place to visit?'

'It's not too bad.'

'Any hotels?'

'Quite a few. But at this time of year they're pretty quiet.'

'So I'd have no problem getting a room if I were to go up there to visit a. . .friend?'

Courtenay felt as if her heart was going to explode with joy. 'No problem at all.'

'Good. I shall plan on going up there very soon. And very often.' The words were casually spoken, but they held a solemn promise. 'Isn't it a wonderful day?'

'It is indeed. . .a perfect day!'

'I thought I'd go for a hike along the beach.' Graydon raked his hand through his tousled black hair, the masculine gesture tugging at Courtenay's heartstrings, then he paused for a beat before saying, in a suddenly grave tone, 'Courtenay West, would you like to walk with me?'

'Yes,' Courtenay said, 'I will walk with you.' She knew what he was really asking.

Side by side, they strolled along the water's edge. She noticed that he didn't touch her, didn't even put an easy arm around her shoulder, and she knew why not. Just as she knew deep in her heart that the day would come when he would.

For now, just the joy of being together, and getting to know each other, was enough.

Mills & Boon

SEPTEMBER 1991 HARDBACK TITLES

ROMANCE

MASQUERADE *Historical*

MEDICAL ROMANCE

LARGE PRINT

Mills & Boon

OCTOBER 1991 HARDBACK TITLES

─── ROMANCE ───

The Stone Princess *Robyn Donald*	3572	0 263 12922 5
Safety in Numbers *Sandra Field*	3573	0 263 12923 3
Reluctant Mistress *Natalie Fox*	3574	0 263 12924 1
Leader of the Pack *Catherine George*	3575	0 263 12925 X
Loveable Katie Lovewell *Emma Goldrick*	3576	0 263 12926 8
Goodbye Delaney *Kay Gregory*	3577	0 263 12927 6
The Trouble with Love *Jessica Hart*	3578	0 263 12928 4
Two-Faced Woman *Roberta Leigh*	3579	0 263 12929 2
Silver Lady *Mary Lyons*	3580	0 263 12930 6
Diamond Fire *Anne Mather*	3581	0 263 12931 4
Tired of Kissing *Annabel Murray*	3582	0 263 12932 2
A Stranger's Trust *Emma Richmond*	3583	0 263 12933 0
His Woman *Jessica Steele*	3584	0 263 12934 9
The Golden Greek *Sally Wentworth*	3585	0 263 12935 7
Devon's Desire *Quinn Wilder*	3586	0 263 12936 5
Shadow Heart *Cathy Williams*	3587	0 263 12937 3

MASQUERADE *Historical*

Mr Ravensworth's Ward *Petra Nash*	M273	0 263 13042 8
Hearts of the Vendee *Truda Taylor*	M274	0 263 13043 6

MEDICAL ROMANCE

All for Love *Margaret Barker*	D191	0 263 13048 7
Hometown Hospital *Lydia Balmain*	D192	0 263 13049 5

LARGE PRINT

Passionate Betrayal *Jacqueline Baird*	463	0 263 12801 6
A Promise to Repay *Amanda Browning*	464	0 263 12802 4
Happy Ending *Sandra Field*	465	0 263 12803 2
An Unequal Partnership *Rosemary Gibson*	466	0 263 12804 0
Shotgun Wedding *Charlotte Lamb*	467	0 263 12805 9
That Long-Ago Summer *Sandra Marton*	468	0 263 12806 7
Such Sweet Poison *Anne Mather*	469	0 263 12807 5
Perilous Refuge *Patricia Wilson*	470	0 263 12808 3